Duncan & Mallory

By Robert Asprin and Mel. White

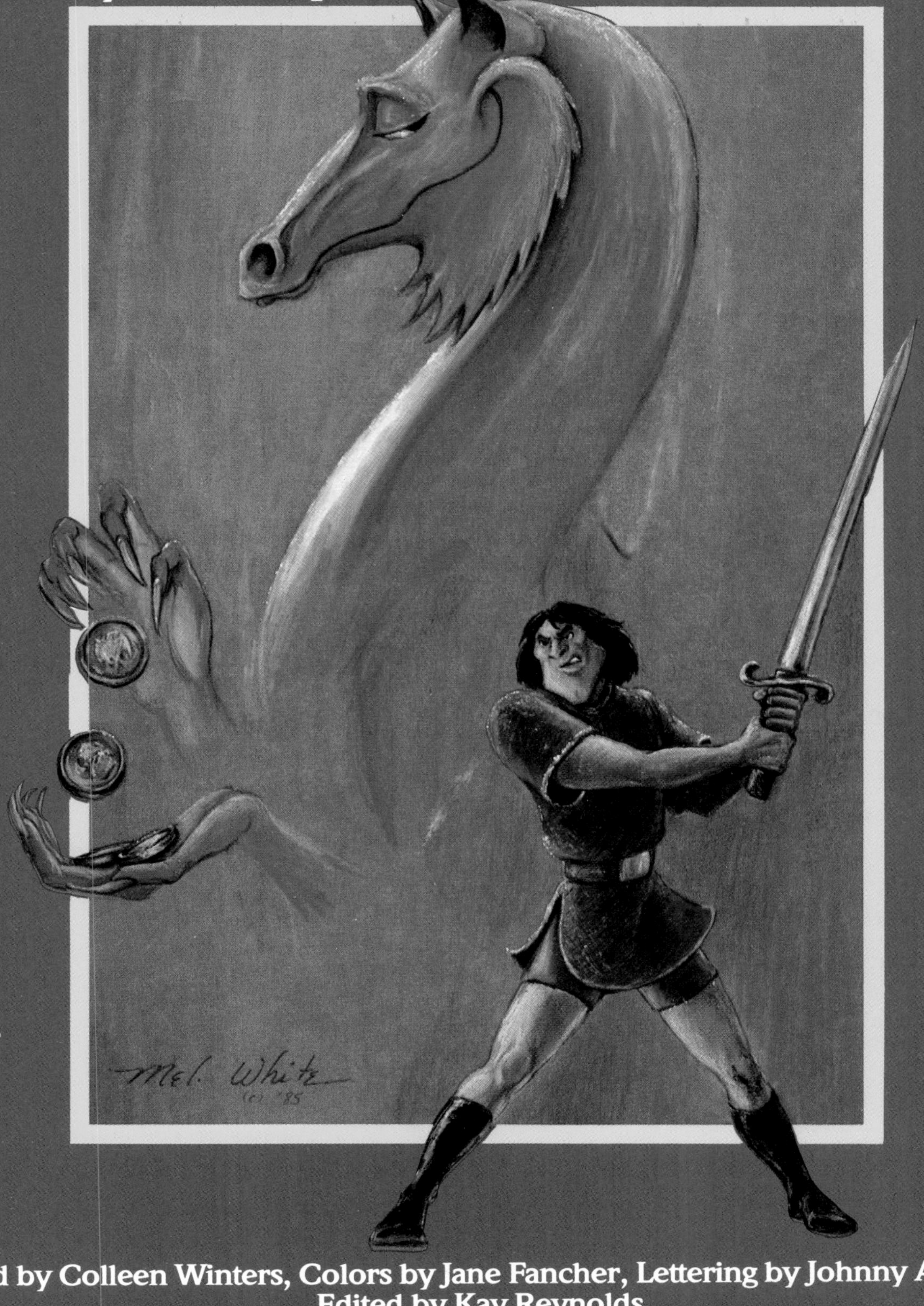
Mel. White
(c) '85

Inked by Colleen Winters, Colors by Jane Fancher, Lettering by Johnny Amburn
Edited by Kay Reynolds

THE DONNING COMPANY/PUBLISHERS • NORFOLK/VIRGINIA BEACH • 1986

Duncan & Mallory is one of the many graphic novels published by The Donning Company/Publishers. For a complete listing of our titles, please write to the address below.

The Donning Company/Publishers
5659 Virginia Beach Boulevard
Norfolk, Virginia 23502

0 9 8 7 6 5 4 3 2 1

Library of Congress Cataloging-in-Publication Data:

Asprin, Robert.
    Duncan and Mallory.
    I. White, Mel., 1949-   . II. Title.
PN6727.A76D86   1986   741.5'973   86-4488
ISBN 0-89865-456-4 (pbk.:v. 1)

Printed in the United States of America

Duncan & Mallory

ROBERT ASPRIN & MEL. WHITE

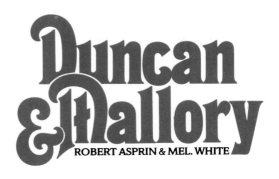

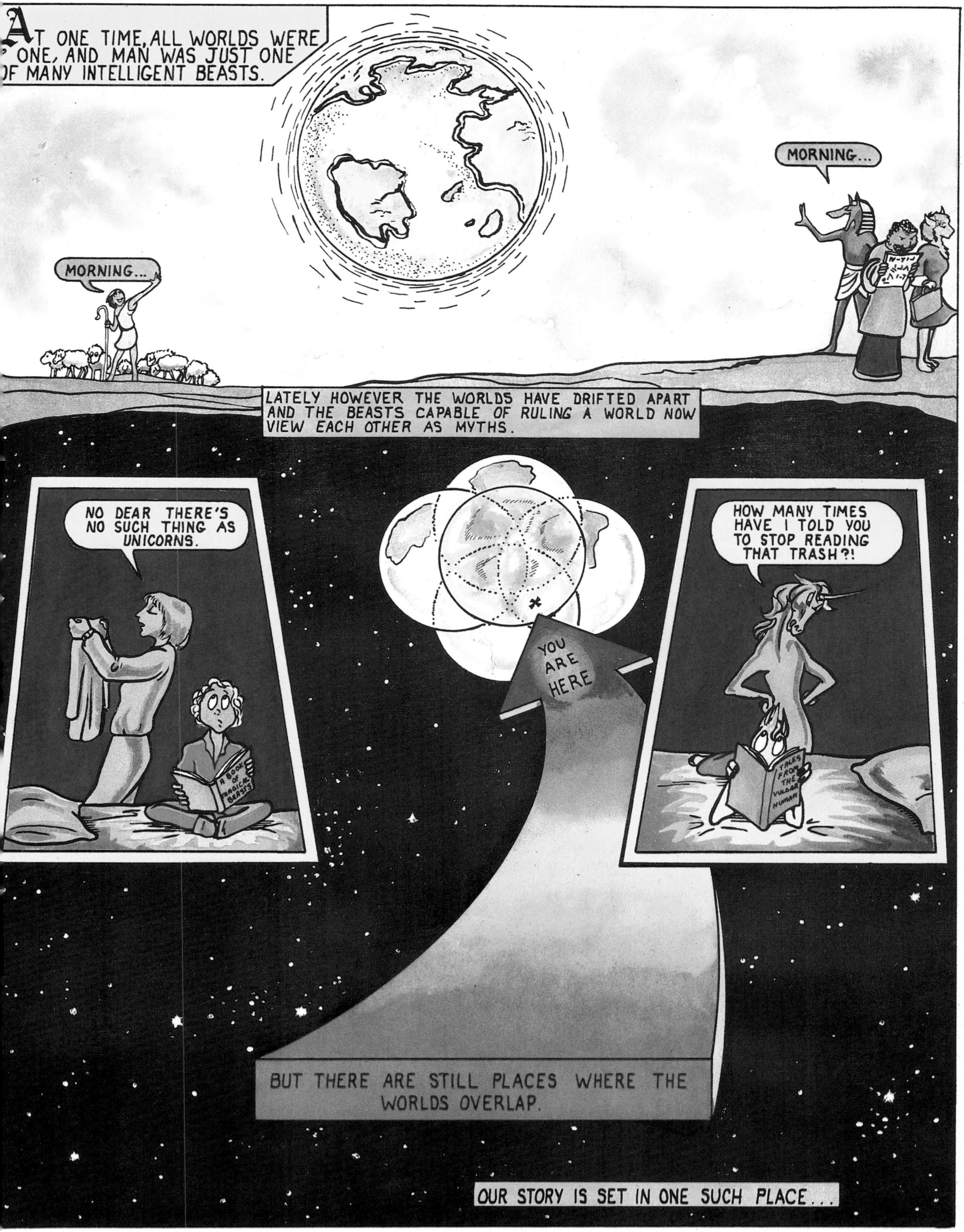
AT ONE TIME, ALL WORLDS WERE ONE, AND MAN WAS JUST ONE OF MANY INTELLIGENT BEASTS.
MORNING...
MORNING...
LATELY HOWEVER THE WORLDS HAVE DRIFTED APART AND THE BEASTS CAPABLE OF RULING A WORLD NOW VIEW EACH OTHER AS MYTHS.
NO DEAR THERE'S NO SUCH THING AS UNICORNS.
A BOOK OF MAGICAL BEASTS
YOU ARE HERE
HOW MANY TIMES HAVE I TOLD YOU TO STOP READING THAT TRASH?!
TALES FROM THE VULGAR HUMAN
BUT THERE ARE STILL PLACES WHERE THE WORLDS OVERLAP.
OUR STORY IS SET IN ONE SUCH PLACE...

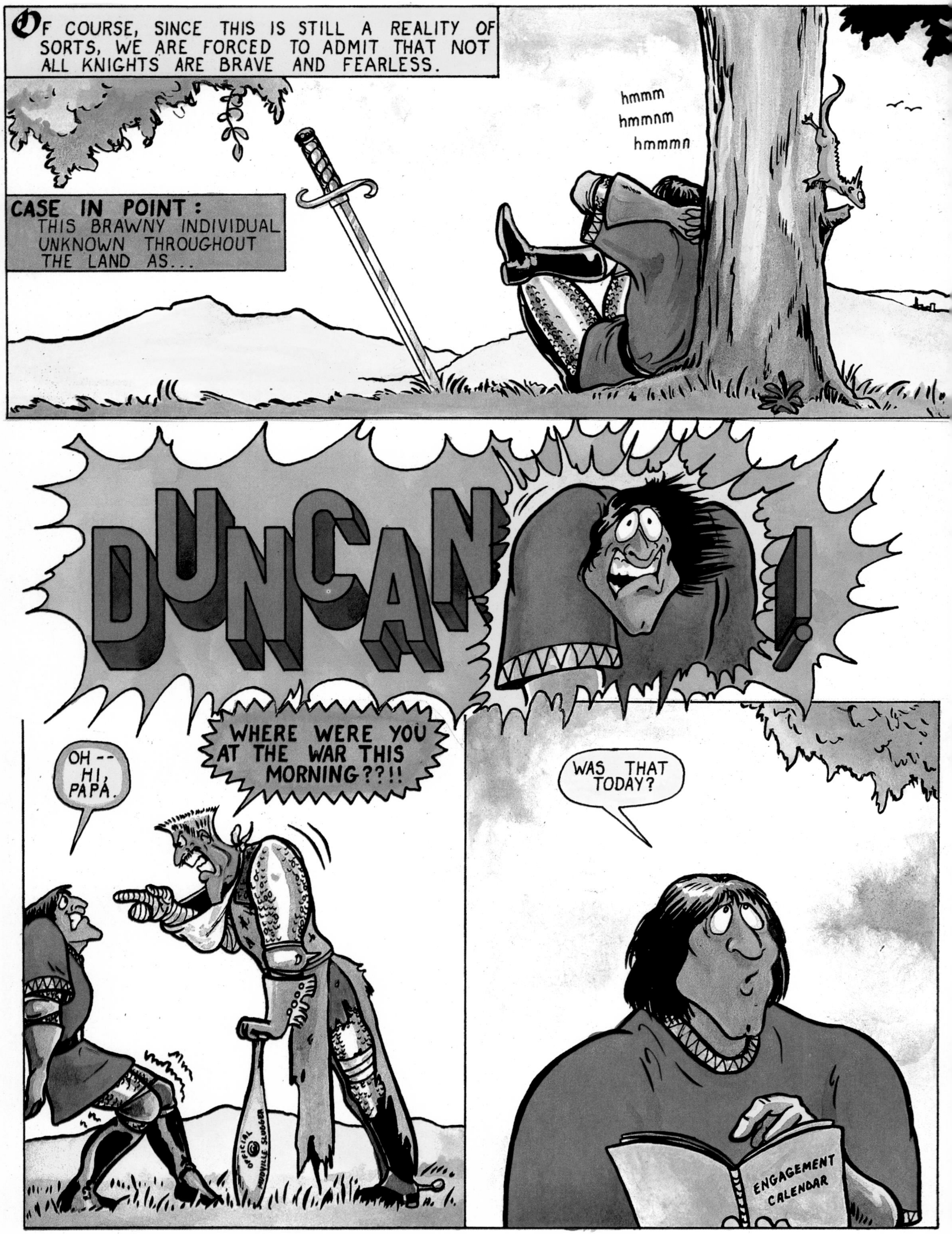

OF COURSE, SINCE THIS IS STILL A REALITY OF SORTS, WE ARE FORCED TO ADMIT THAT NOT ALL KNIGHTS ARE BRAVE AND FEARLESS.
hmmm
hmmnm
hmmmn
CASE IN POINT: THIS BRAWNY INDIVIDUAL UNKNOWN THROUGHOUT THE LAND AS...
DUNCAN!
OH -- HI, PAPA.
WHERE WERE YOU AT THE WAR THIS MORNING??!!
OFFICIAL MUDVILLE SLUGGER
WAS THAT TODAY?
ENGAGEMENT CALENDAR

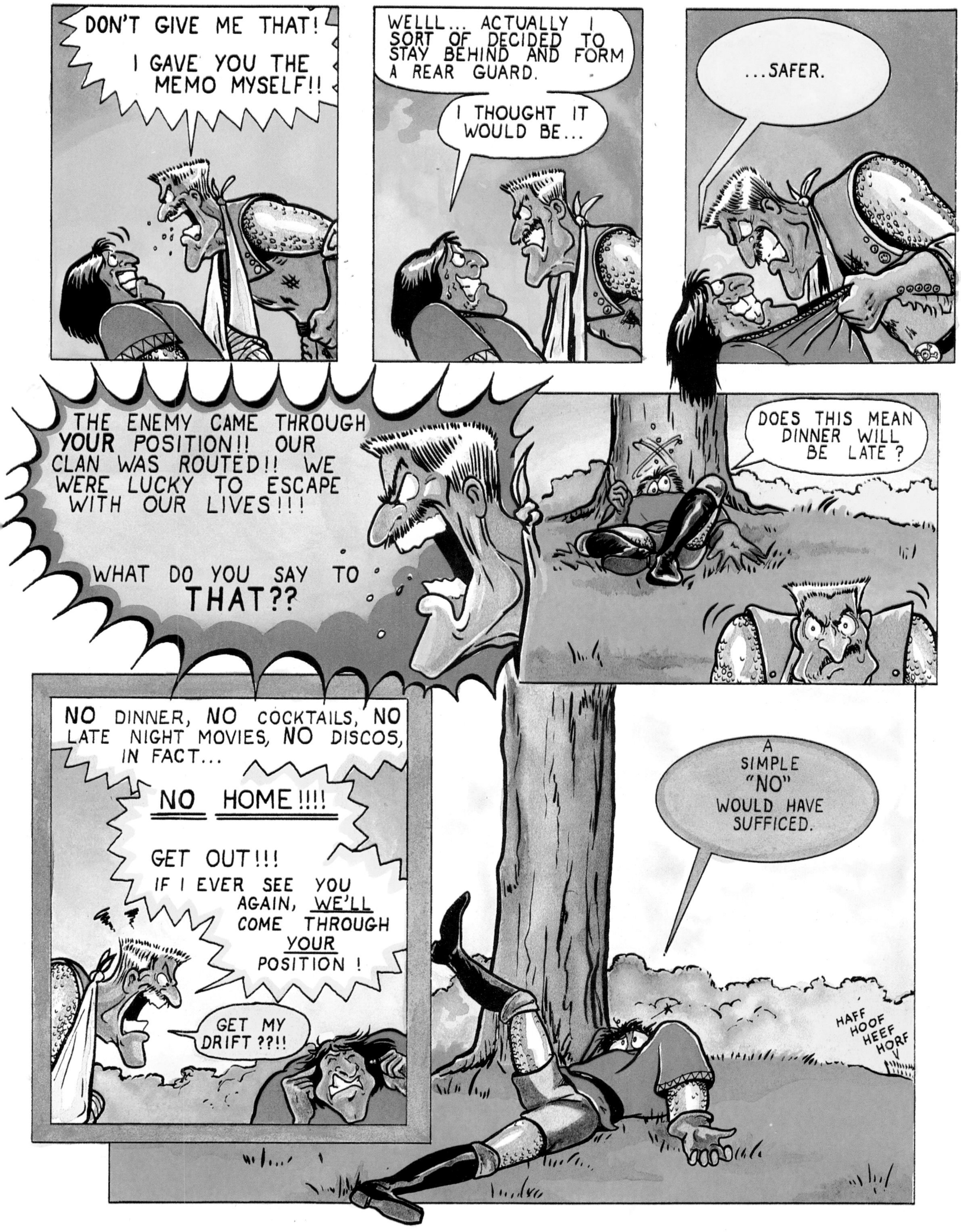

DON'T GIVE ME THAT!
I GAVE YOU THE MEMO MYSELF!!
WELLL... ACTUALLY I SORT OF DECIDED TO STAY BEHIND AND FORM A REAR GUARD.
I THOUGHT IT WOULD BE...
...SAFER.
THE ENEMY CAME THROUGH YOUR POSITION!! OUR CLAN WAS ROUTED!! WE WERE LUCKY TO ESCAPE WITH OUR LIVES!!!
WHAT DO YOU SAY TO THAT??
DOES THIS MEAN DINNER WILL BE LATE?
NO DINNER, NO COCKTAILS, NO LATE NIGHT MOVIES, NO DISCOS, IN FACT...
NO HOME!!!!
GET OUT!!!
IF I EVER SEE YOU AGAIN, WE'LL COME THROUGH YOUR POSITION!
GET MY DRIFT??!!
A SIMPLE "NO" WOULD HAVE SUFFICED.
HAFF HOOF HEEF HORF

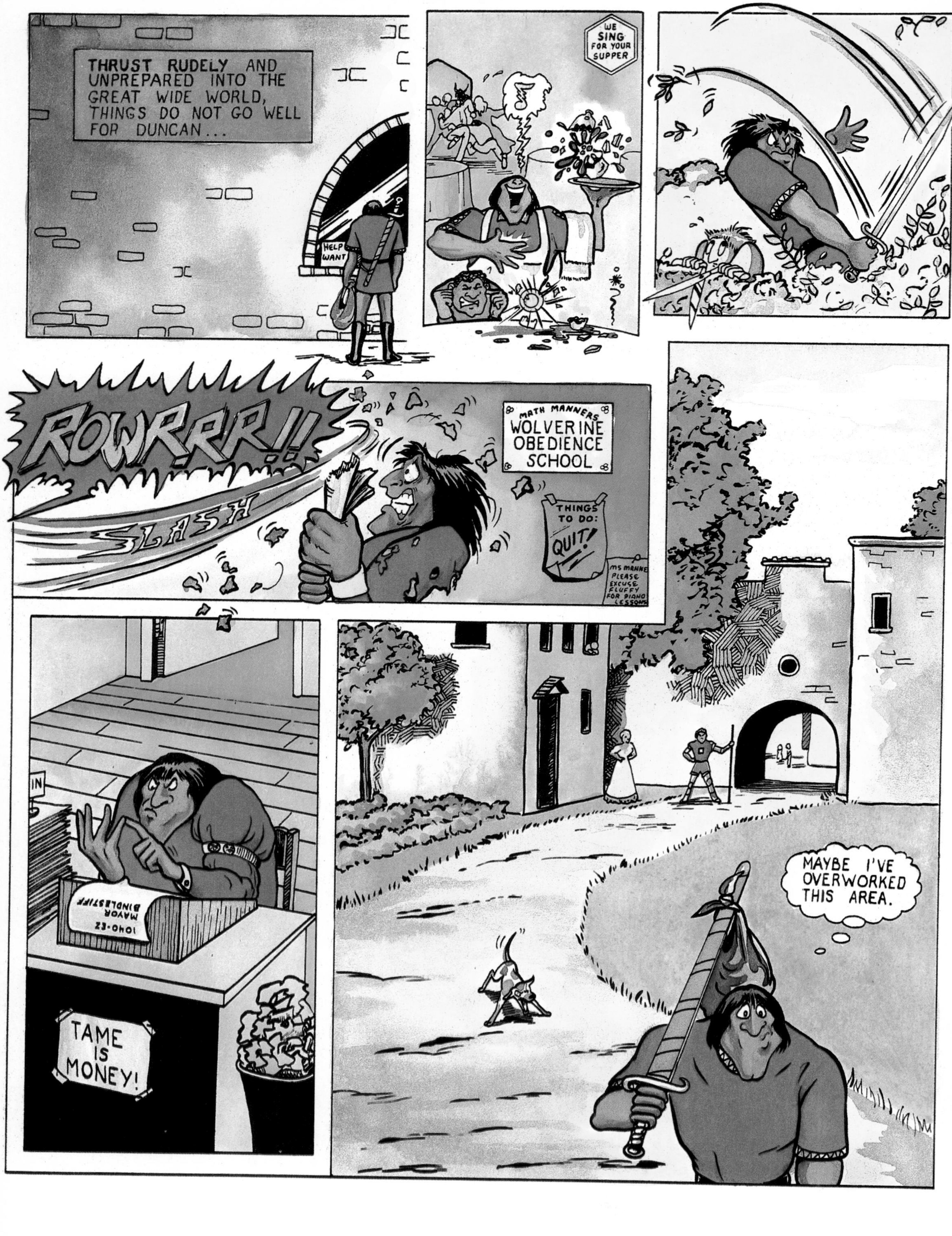
THRUST RUDELY AND UNPREPARED INTO THE GREAT WIDE WORLD, THINGS DO NOT GO WELL FOR DUNCAN...
HELP WANT
WE SING FOR YOUR SUPPER
ROWRRR!!
SLASH
MATH MANNERS
WOLVERINE OBEDIENCE SCHOOL
THINGS TO DO: QUIT!
MS MANNE PLEASE EXCUSE FLUFFY FOR PIANO LESSONS
IN
MAYOR BINDLESTIFF
TAME IS MONEY!
MAYBE I'VE OVERWORKED THIS AREA.

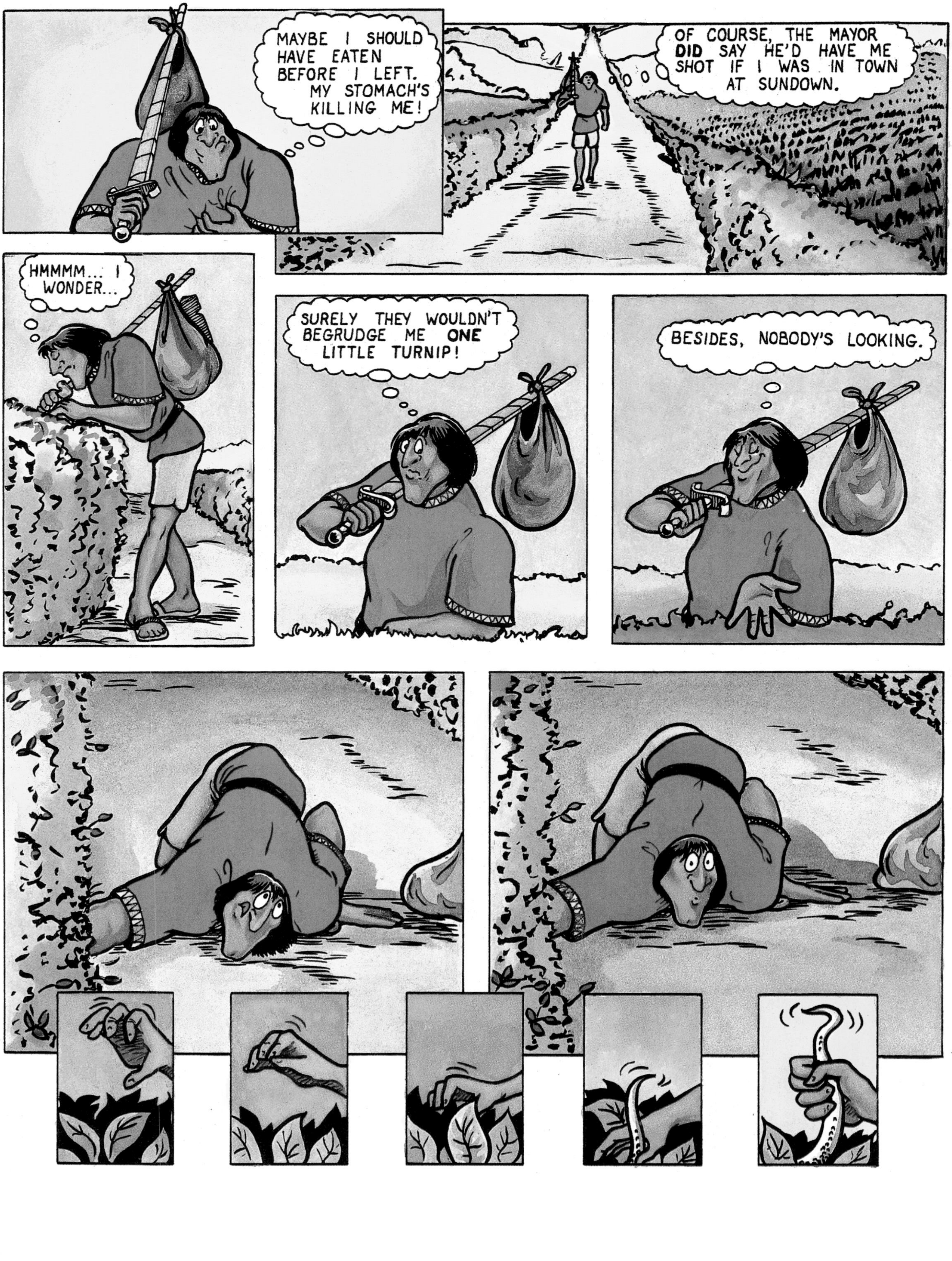
MAYBE I SHOULD HAVE EATEN BEFORE I LEFT. MY STOMACH'S KILLING ME!
OF COURSE, THE MAYOR **DID** SAY HE'D HAVE ME SHOT IF I WAS IN TOWN AT SUNDOWN.
HMMMM... I WONDER...
SURELY THEY WOULDN'T BEGRUDGE ME **ONE** LITTLE TURNIP!
BESIDES, NOBODY'S LOOKING.

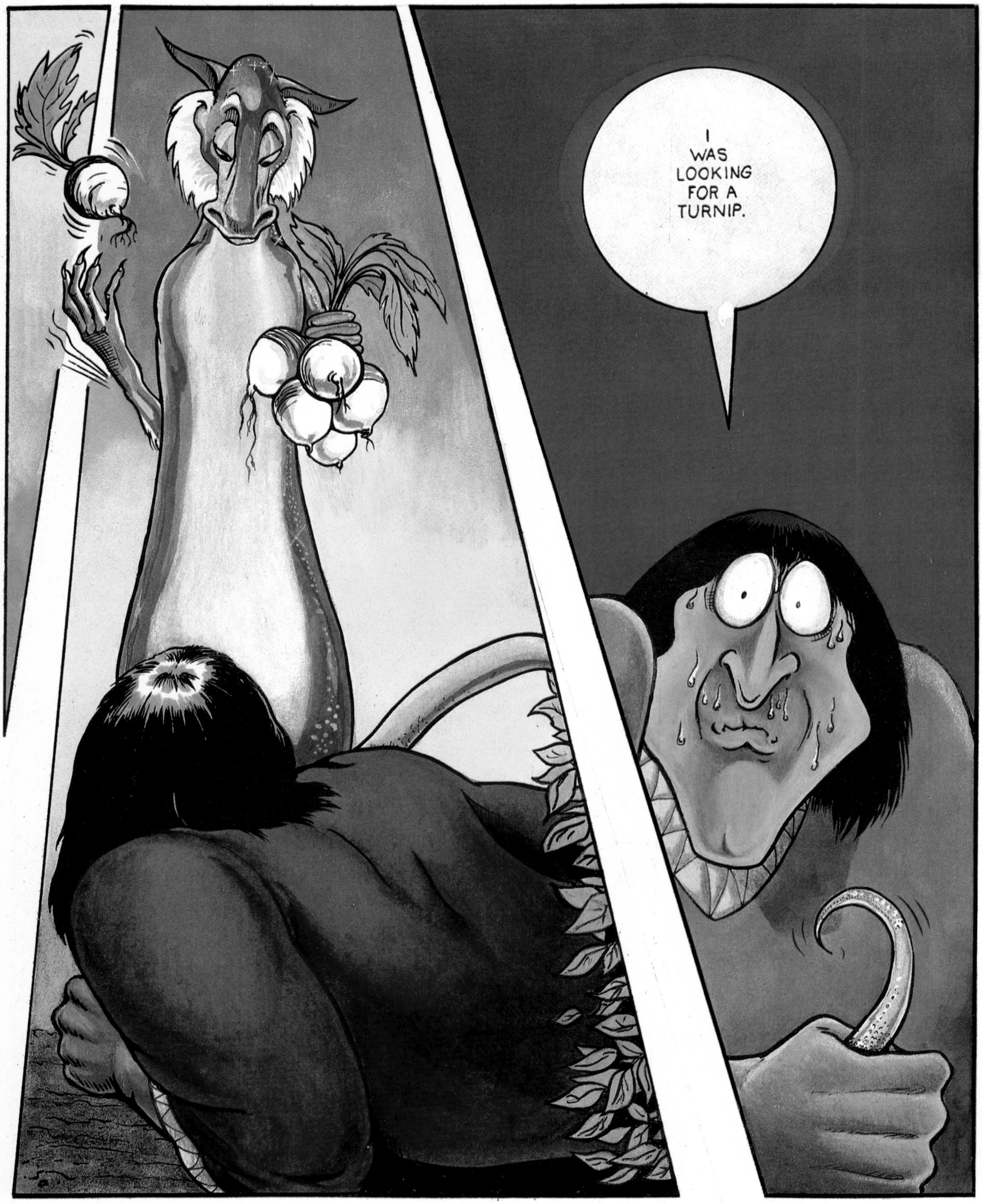
I WAS LOOKING FOR A TURNIP.

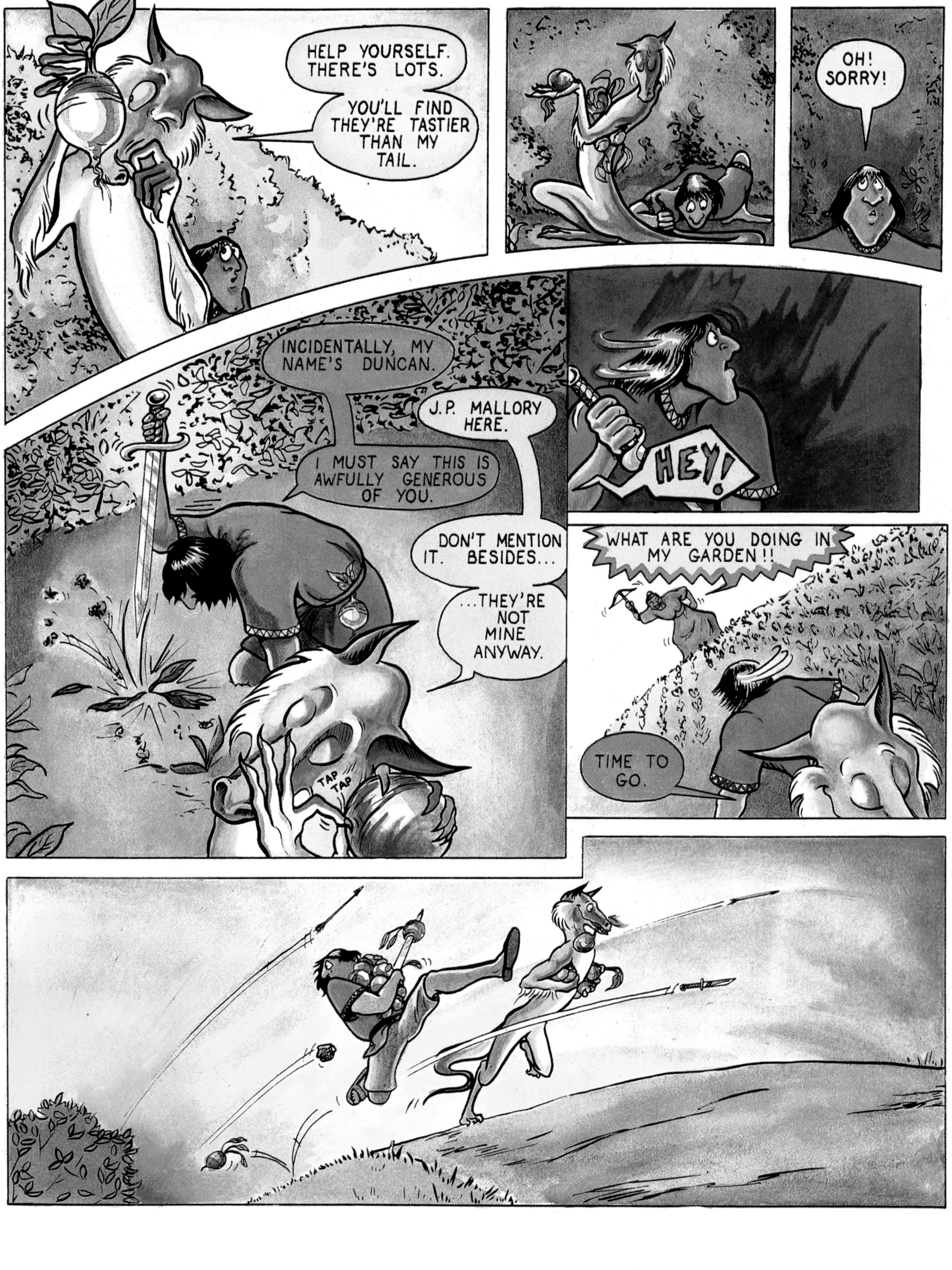
HELP YOURSELF. THERE'S LOTS.
YOU'LL FIND THEY'RE TASTIER THAN MY TAIL.
OH! SORRY!
INCIDENTALLY, MY NAME'S DUNCAN.
J.P. MALLORY HERE.
I MUST SAY THIS IS AWFULLY GENEROUS OF YOU.
DON'T MENTION IT. BESIDES...
...THEY'RE NOT MINE ANYWAY.
TAP TAP
HEY!
WHAT ARE YOU DOING IN MY GARDEN!!
TIME TO GO.

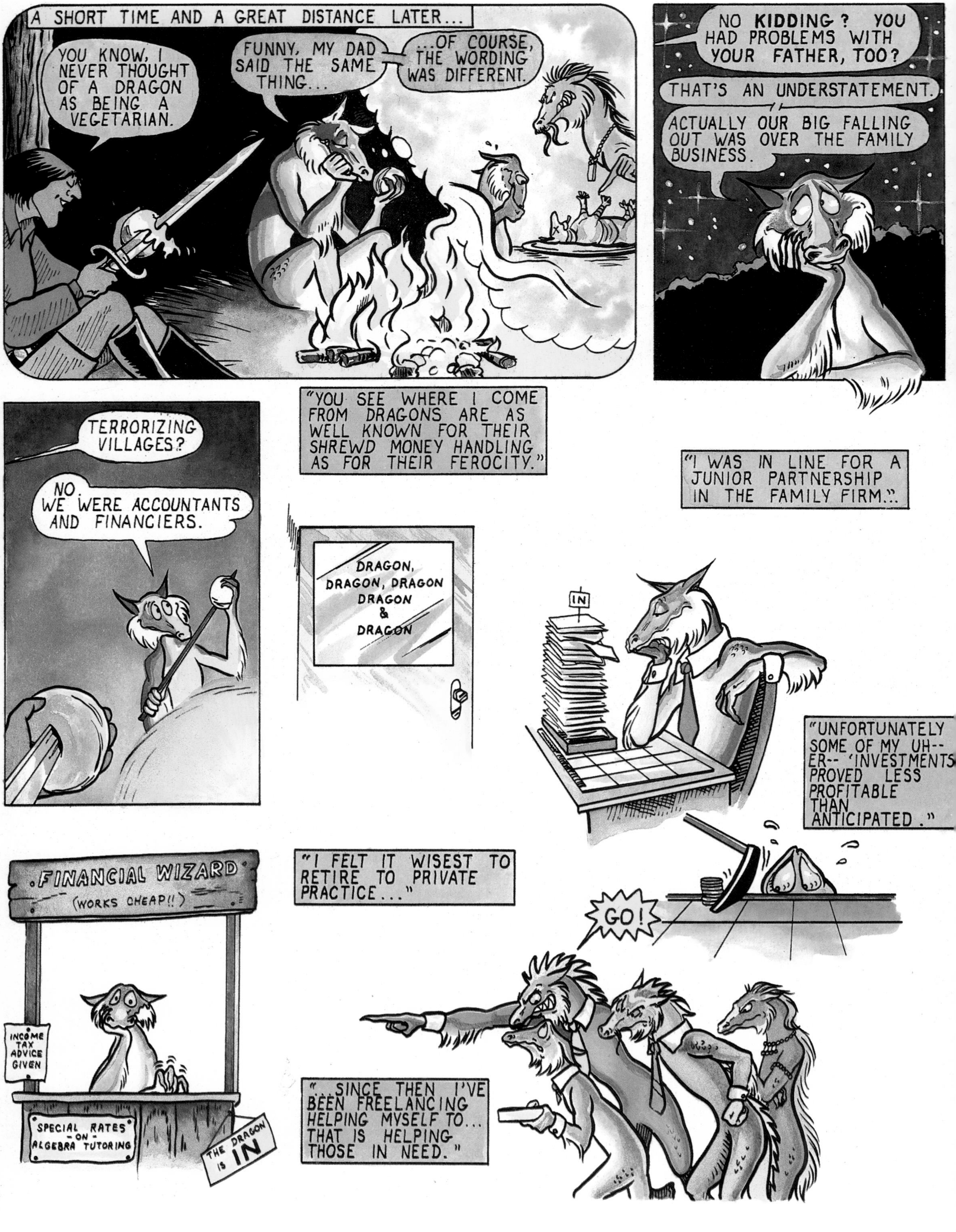
A SHORT TIME AND A GREAT DISTANCE LATER...
YOU KNOW, I NEVER THOUGHT OF A DRAGON AS BEING A VEGETARIAN.
FUNNY, MY DAD SAID THE SAME THING...
...OF COURSE, THE WORDING WAS DIFFERENT.
NO KIDDING? YOU HAD PROBLEMS WITH YOUR FATHER, TOO?
THAT'S AN UNDERSTATEMENT.
ACTUALLY OUR BIG FALLING OUT WAS OVER THE FAMILY BUSINESS.
TERRORIZING VILLAGES?
NO. WE WERE ACCOUNTANTS AND FINANCIERS.
"YOU SEE WHERE I COME FROM DRAGONS ARE AS WELL KNOWN FOR THEIR SHREWD MONEY HANDLING AS FOR THEIR FEROCITY."
DRAGON, DRAGON, DRAGON DRAGON & DRAGON
"I WAS IN LINE FOR A JUNIOR PARTNERSHIP IN THE FAMILY FIRM..."
IN
"UNFORTUNATELY SOME OF MY UH-- ER-- 'INVESTMENTS' PROVED LESS PROFITABLE THAN ANTICIPATED."
GO!
FINANCIAL WIZARD
(WORKS CHEAP!!)
INCOME TAX ADVICE GIVEN
SPECIAL RATES -ON- ALGEBRA TUTORING
THE DRAGON IS IN
"I FELT IT WISEST TO RETIRE TO PRIVATE PRACTICE..."
"...SINCE THEN I'VE BEEN FREELANCING HELPING MYSELF TO... THAT IS HELPING THOSE IN NEED."

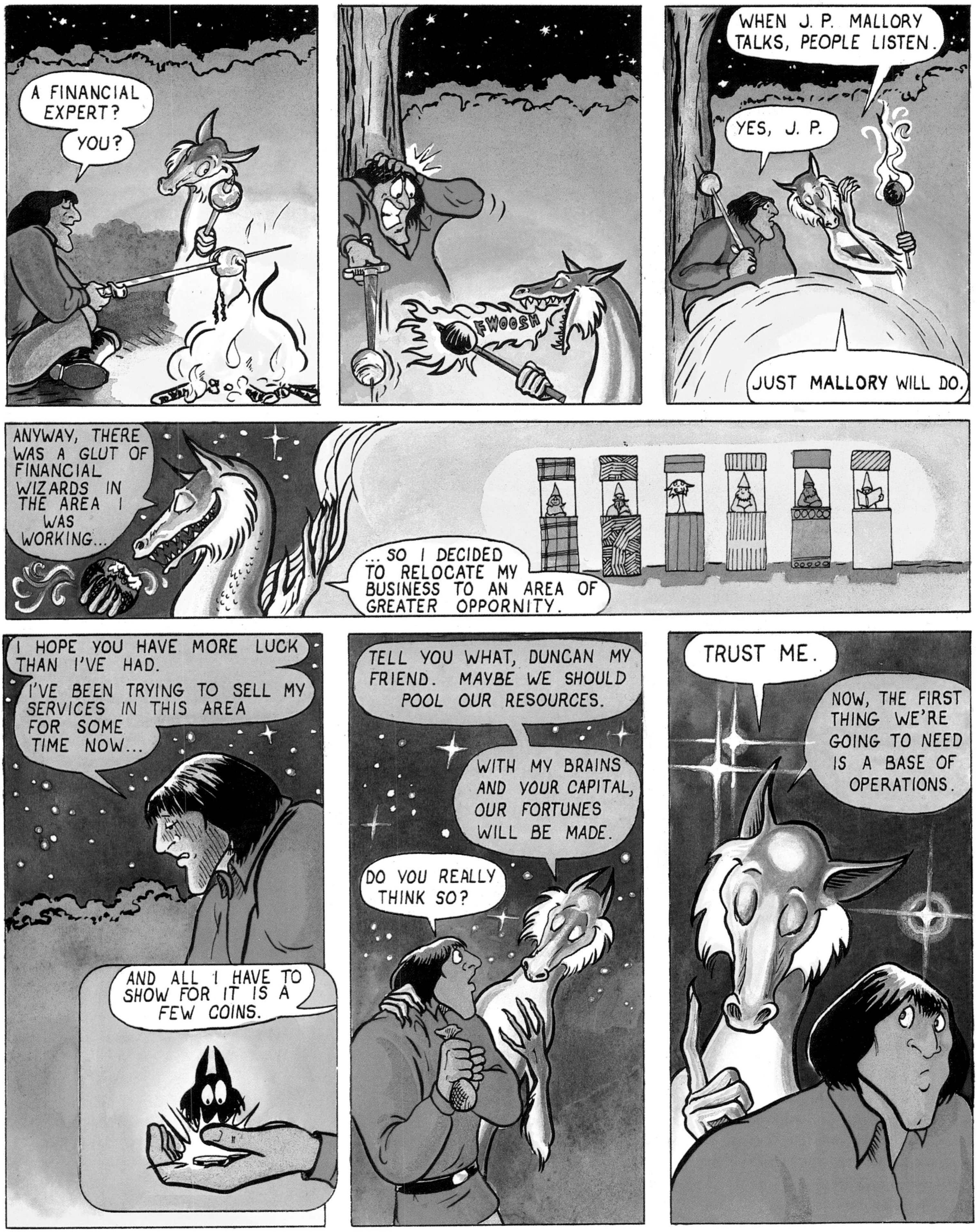
A FINANCIAL EXPERT?
YOU?
FWOOSH
WHEN J. P. MALLORY TALKS, PEOPLE LISTEN.
YES, J. P.
JUST MALLORY WILL DO.
ANYWAY, THERE WAS A GLUT OF FINANCIAL WIZARDS IN THE AREA I WAS WORKING...
...SO I DECIDED TO RELOCATE MY BUSINESS TO AN AREA OF GREATER OPPORNITY.
I HOPE YOU HAVE MORE LUCK THAN I'VE HAD.
I'VE BEEN TRYING TO SELL MY SERVICES IN THIS AREA FOR SOME TIME NOW...
AND ALL I HAVE TO SHOW FOR IT IS A FEW COINS.
TELL YOU WHAT, DUNCAN MY FRIEND. MAYBE WE SHOULD POOL OUR RESOURCES.
WITH MY BRAINS AND YOUR CAPITAL, OUR FORTUNES WILL BE MADE.
DO YOU REALLY THINK SO?
TRUST ME.
NOW, THE FIRST THING WE'RE GOING TO NEED IS A BASE OF OPERATIONS.

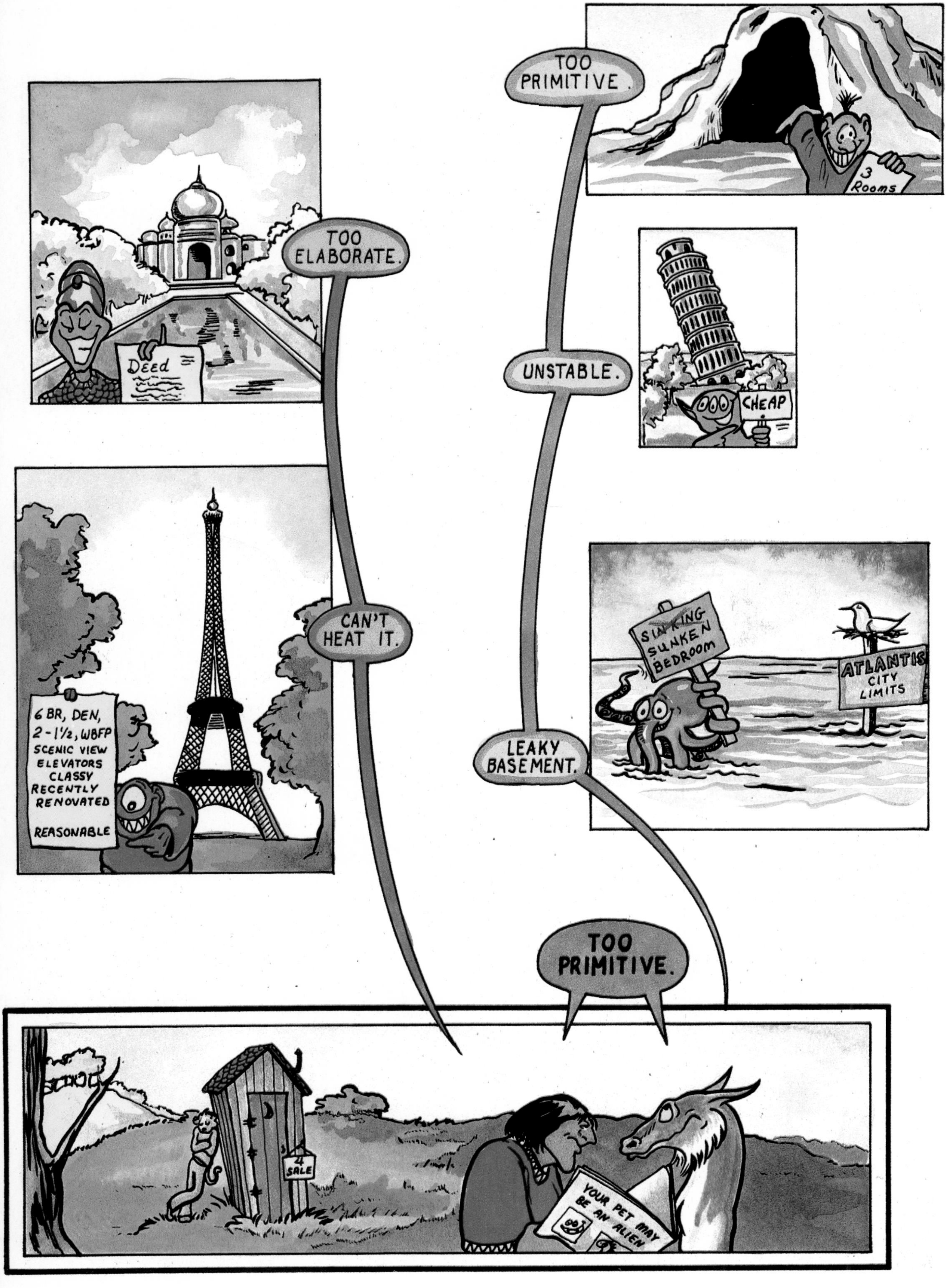
TOO PRIMITIVE.
3 Rooms
TOO ELABORATE.
Deed
UNSTABLE.
CHEAP
CAN'T HEAT IT.
6 BR, DEN, 2 - 1½, WBFP SCENIC VIEW ELEVATORS CLASSY RECENTLY RENOVATED REASONABLE
SINKING SUNKEN BEDROOM
ATLANTIS CITY LIMITS
LEAKY BASEMENT.
TOO PRIMITIVE.
4 SALE
YOUR PET MAY BE AN ALIEN

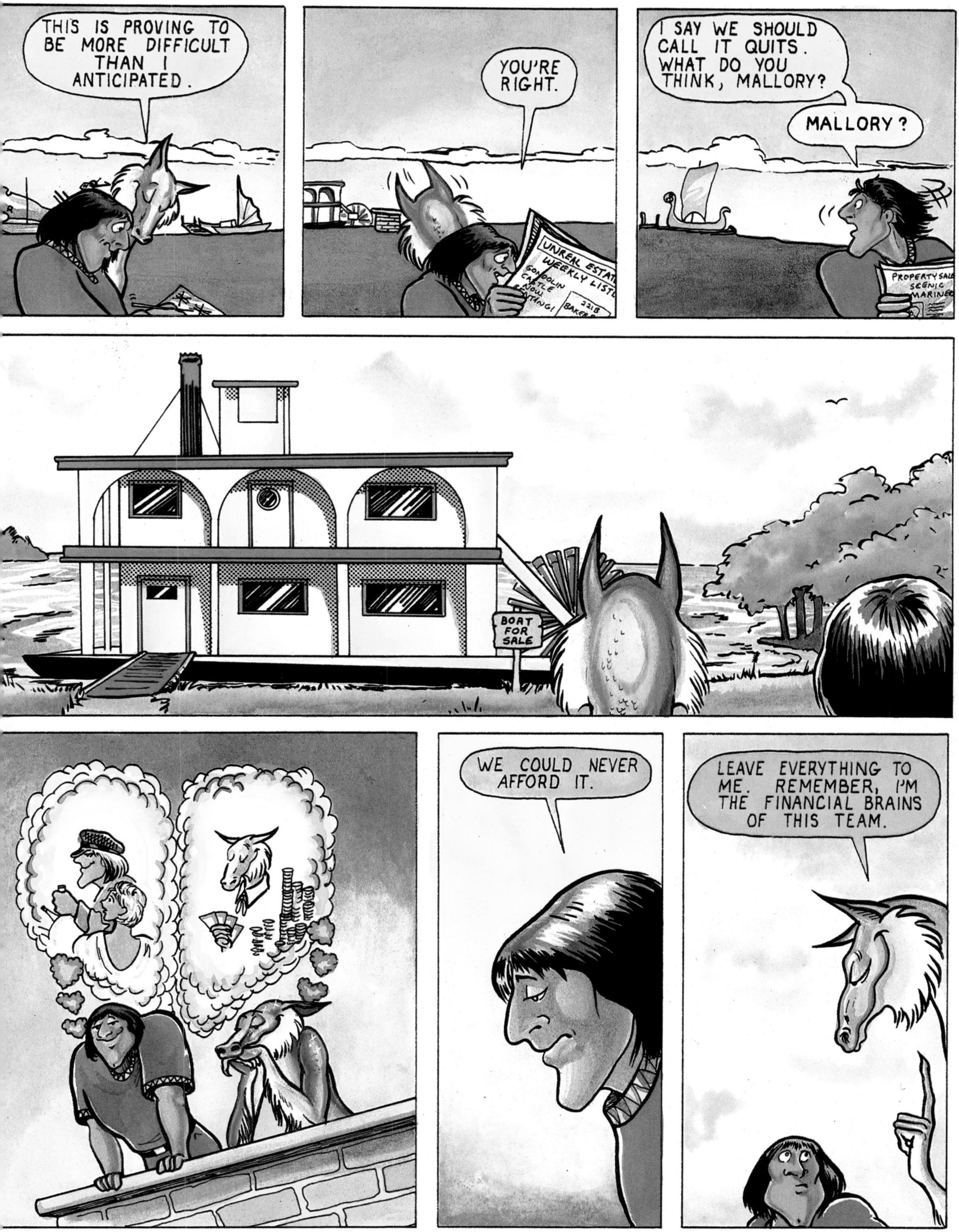
THIS IS PROVING TO BE MORE DIFFICULT THAN I ANTICIPATED.
YOU'RE RIGHT.
I SAY WE SHOULD CALL IT QUITS. WHAT DO YOU THINK, MALLORY?
MALLORY?
BOAT FOR SALE
WE COULD NEVER AFFORD IT.
LEAVE EVERYTHING TO ME. REMEMBER, I'M THE FINANCIAL BRAINS OF THIS TEAM.

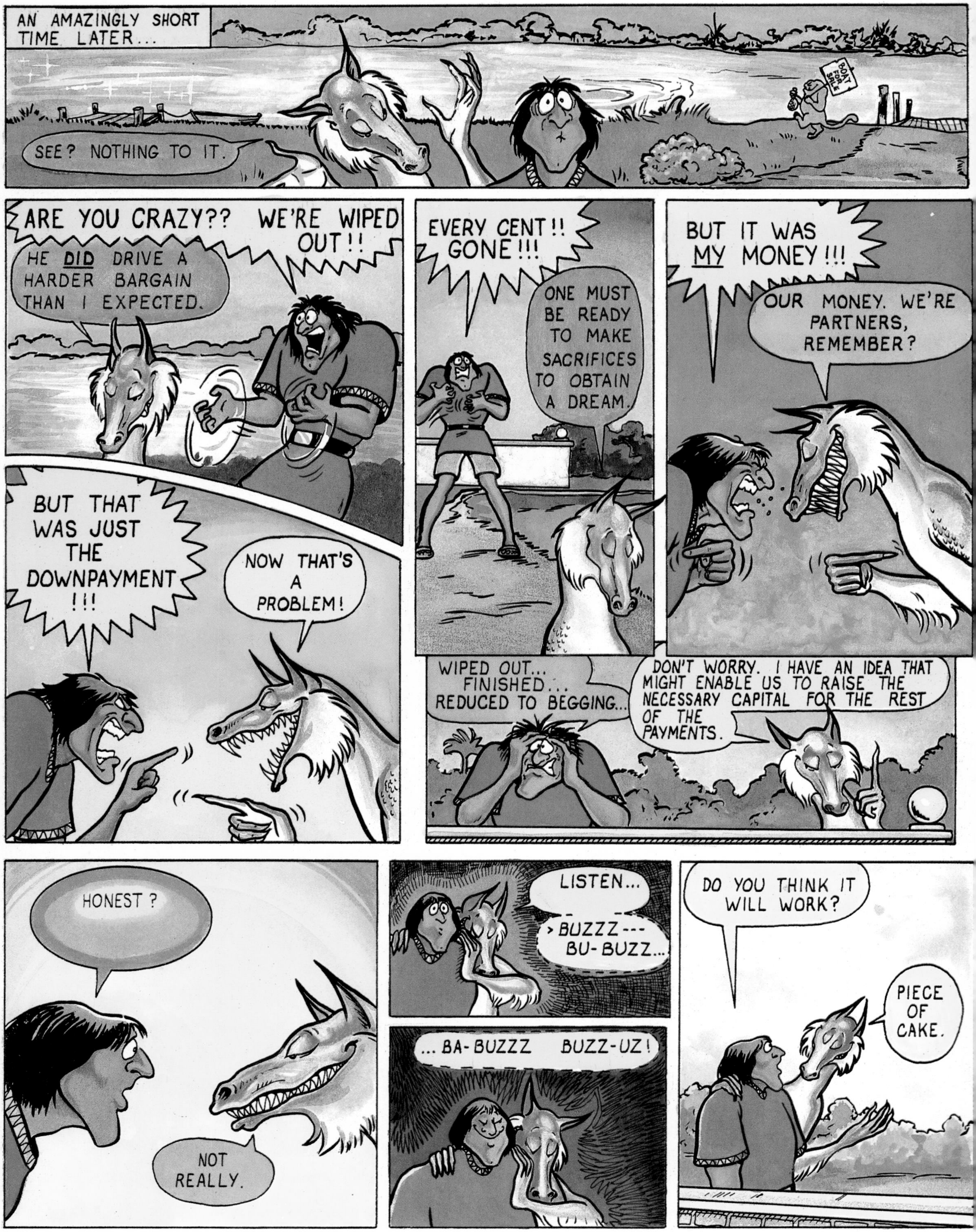
AN AMAZINGLY SHORT TIME LATER...
BOAT FOR SALE
SEE? NOTHING TO IT.
ARE YOU CRAZY?? WE'RE WIPED OUT!!
HE DID DRIVE A HARDER BARGAIN THAN I EXPECTED.
EVERY CENT!! GONE!!!
ONE MUST BE READY TO MAKE SACRIFICES TO OBTAIN A DREAM.
BUT IT WAS MY MONEY!!!
OUR MONEY. WE'RE PARTNERS, REMEMBER?
BUT THAT WAS JUST THE DOWNPAYMENT!!!
NOW THAT'S A PROBLEM!
WIPED OUT... FINISHED... REDUCED TO BEGGING...
DON'T WORRY. I HAVE AN IDEA THAT MIGHT ENABLE US TO RAISE THE NECESSARY CAPITAL FOR THE REST OF THE PAYMENTS.
HONEST?
NOT REALLY.
LISTEN...
BUZZZ--- BU-BUZZ...
...BA-BUZZZ BUZZ-UZ!
DO YOU THINK IT WILL WORK?
PIECE OF CAKE.

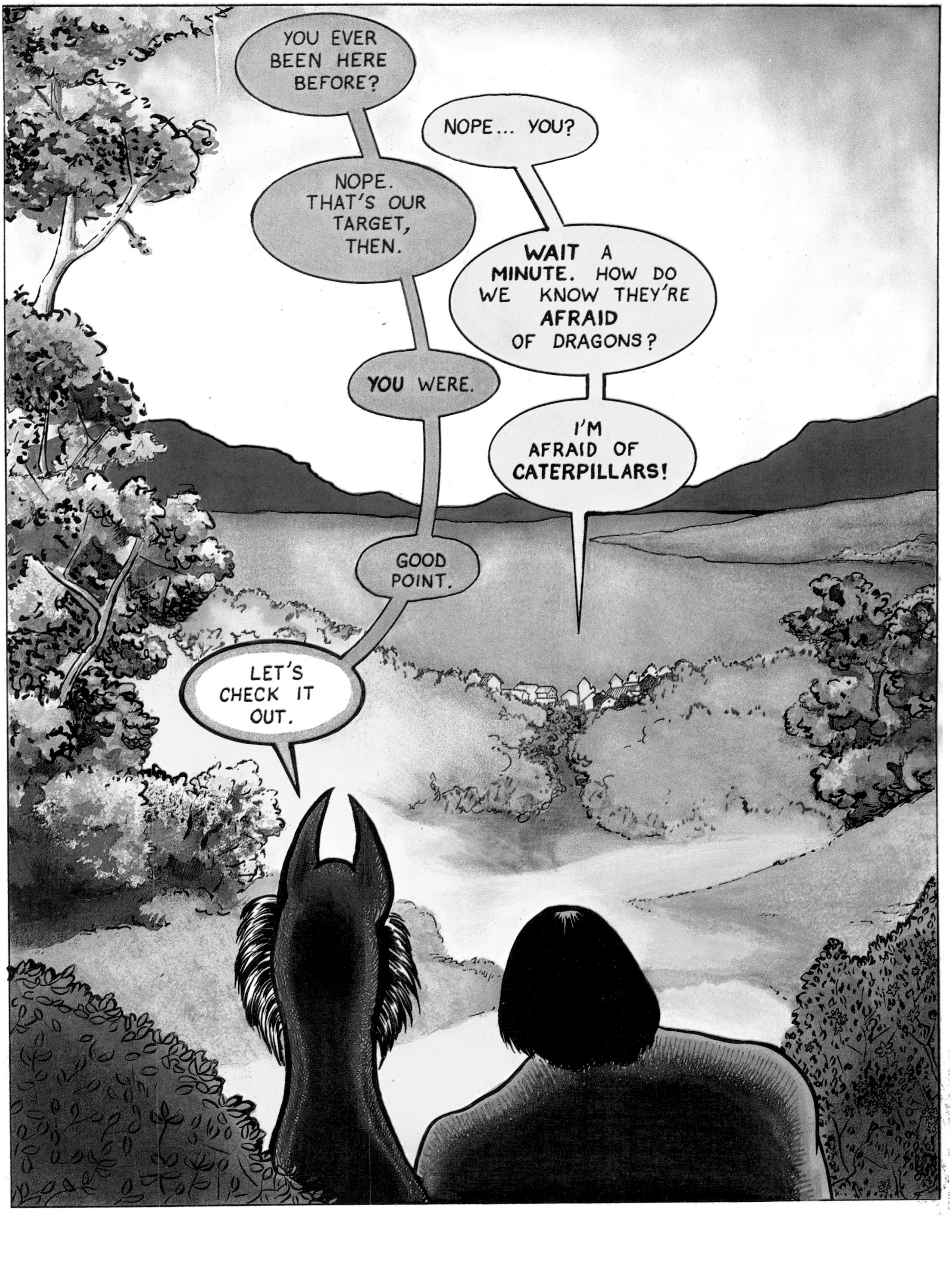
YOU EVER BEEN HERE BEFORE?
NOPE... YOU?
NOPE. THAT'S OUR TARGET, THEN.
WAIT A MINUTE. HOW DO WE KNOW THEY'RE AFRAID OF DRAGONS?
YOU WERE.
I'M AFRAID OF CATERPILLARS!
GOOD POINT.
LET'S CHECK IT OUT.

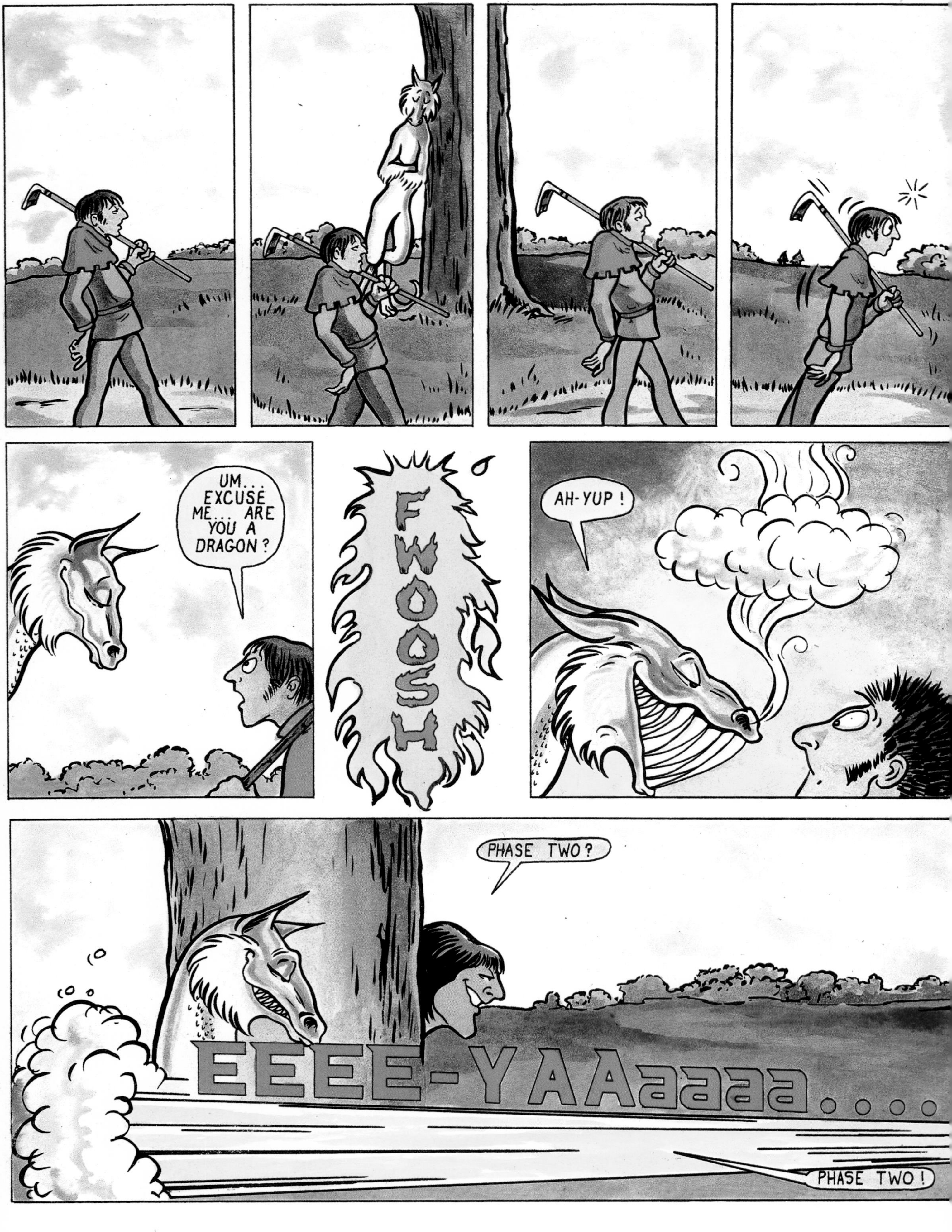

UM... EXCUSE ME... ARE YOU A DRAGON?
FWOOSH
AH-YUP!
PHASE TWO?
EEEE-YAAaaaa....
PHASE TWO!

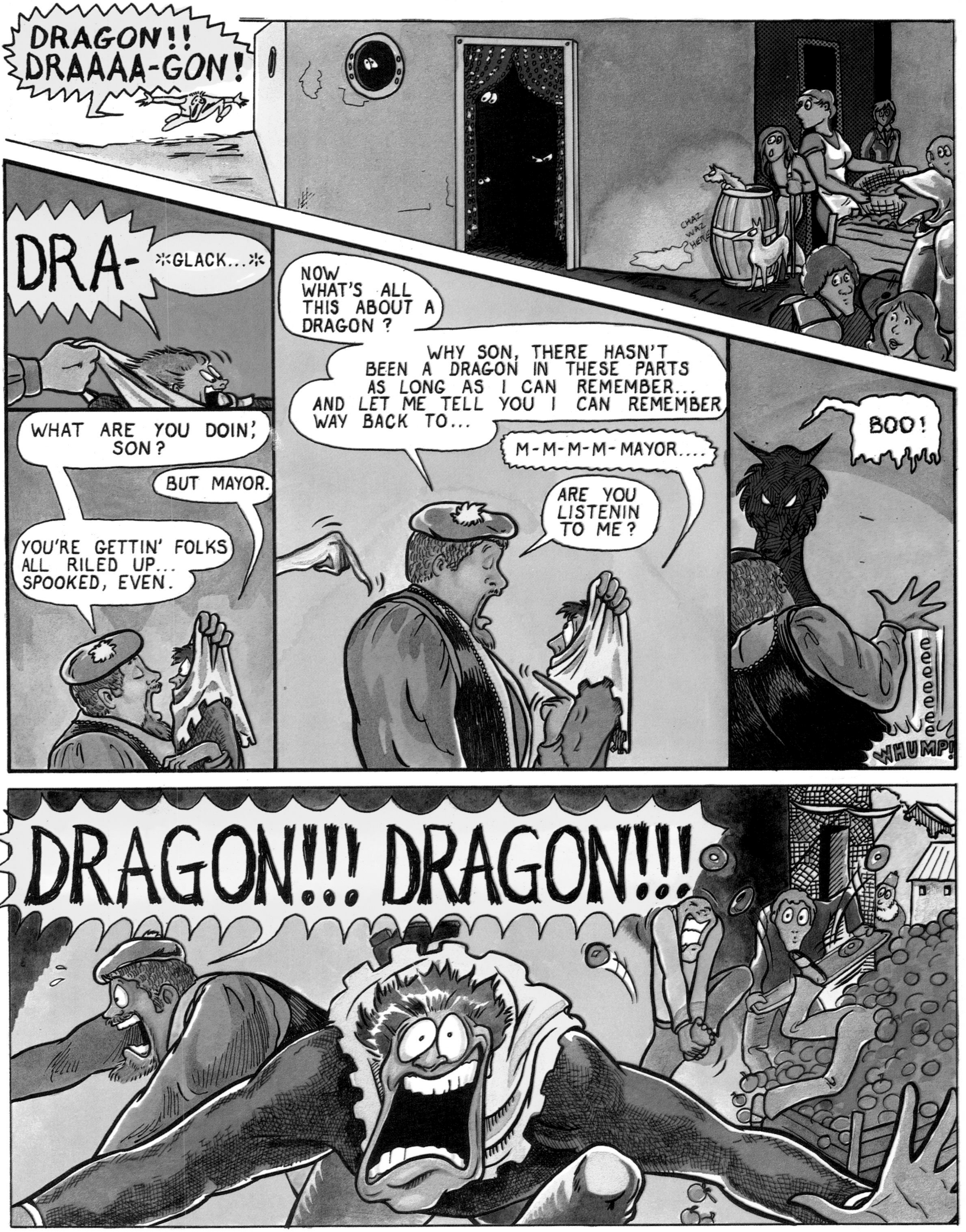
DRAGON!! DRAAAA-GON!
CHAZ WAZ HERE
DRA-
GLACK...
WHAT ARE YOU DOIN', SON?
BUT MAYOR.
YOU'RE GETTIN' FOLKS ALL RILED UP... SPOOKED, EVEN.
NOW WHAT'S ALL THIS ABOUT A DRAGON?
WHY SON, THERE HASN'T BEEN A DRAGON IN THESE PARTS AS LONG AS I CAN REMEMBER... AND LET ME TELL YOU I CAN REMEMBER WAY BACK TO...
M-M-M-M-MAYOR....
ARE YOU LISTENIN TO ME?
BOO!
eeeeeee
WHUMP!
DRAGON!!! DRAGON!!!

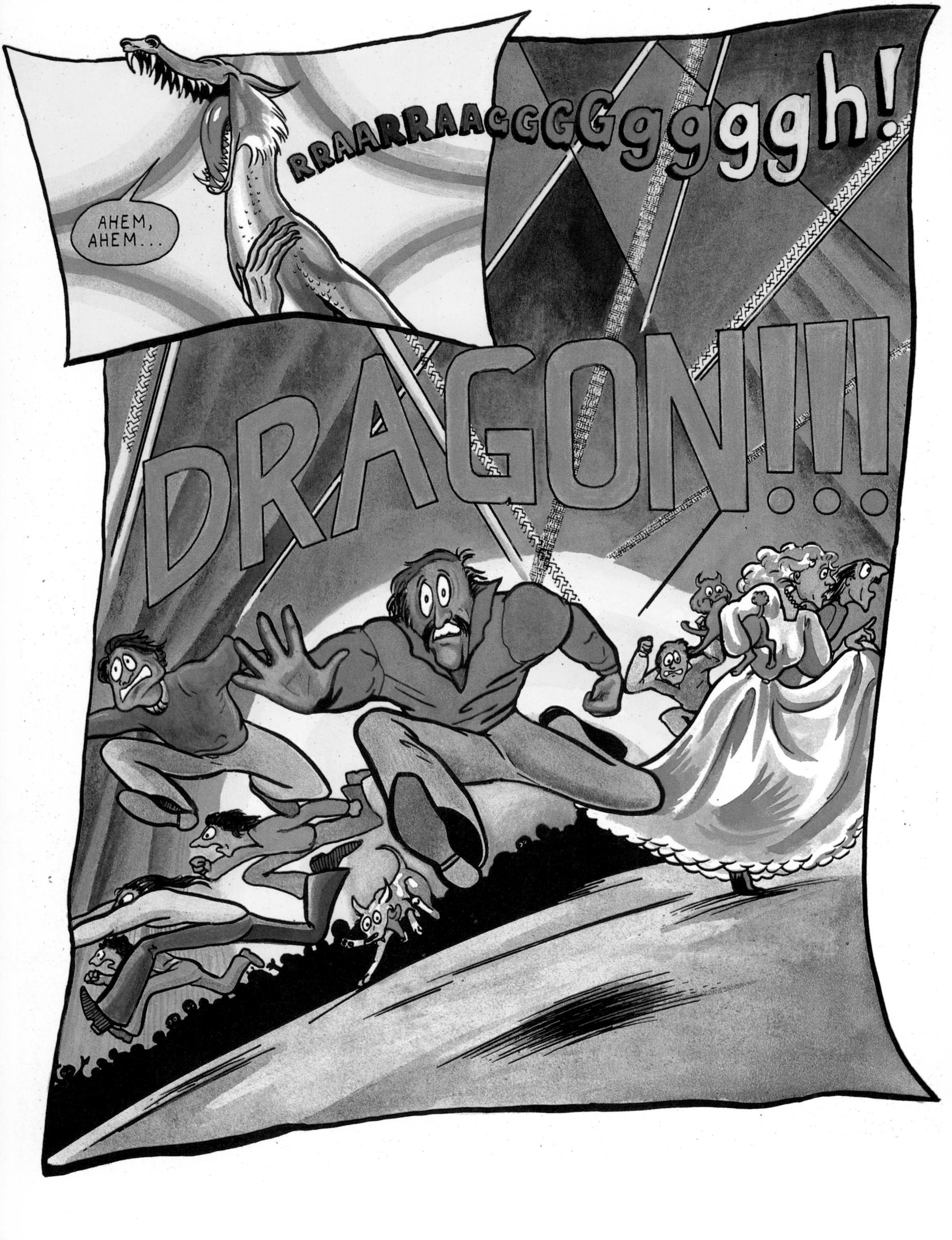
AHEM, AHEM...
RRAARRRAAGGGGggggh!
DRAGON!!!...

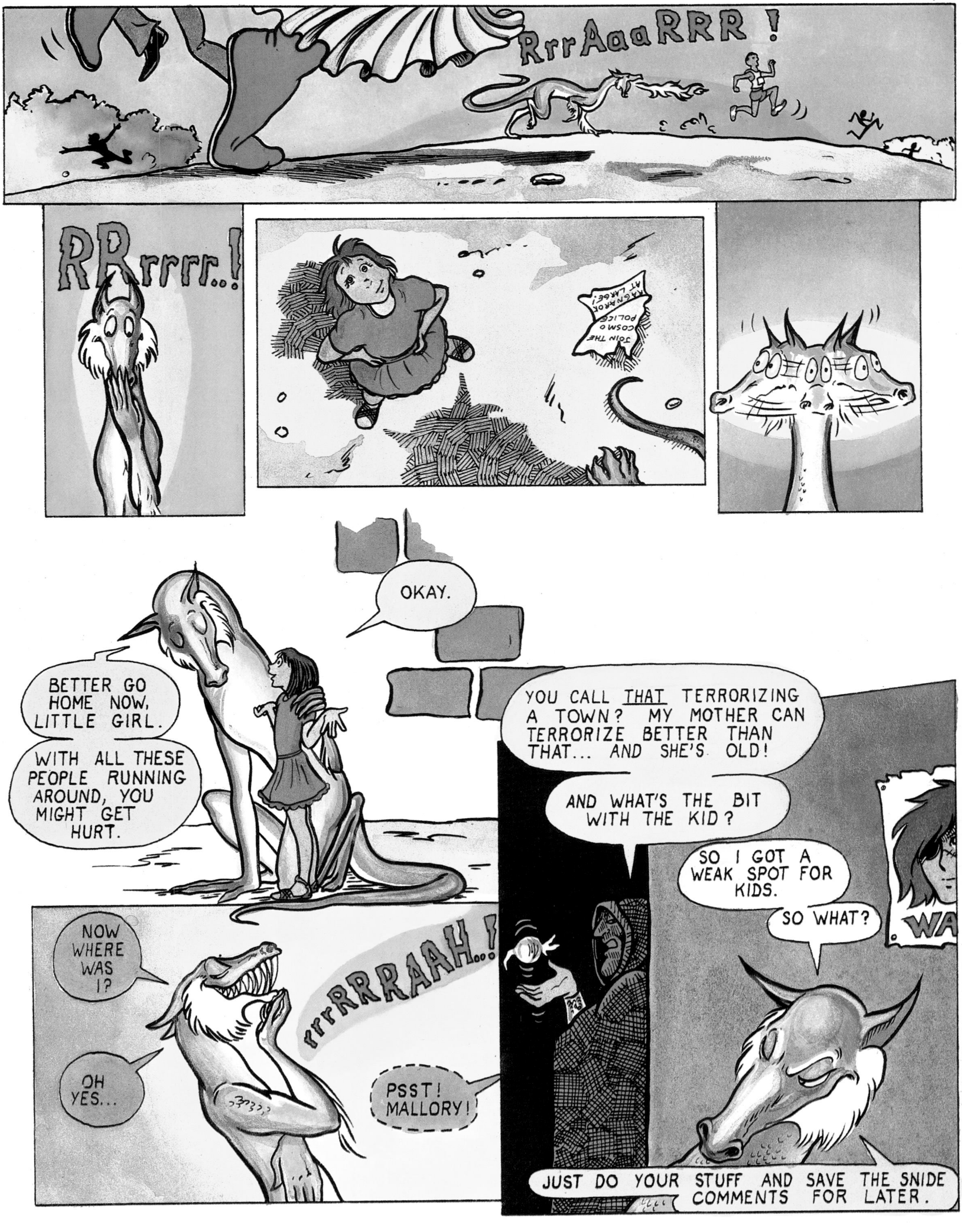
RrrAaaRRR !
RRrrrr..!
JOIN THE COSMO POLICE
RAGNAROK AT LARGE!
OKAY.
BETTER GO HOME NOW, LITTLE GIRL.
WITH ALL THESE PEOPLE RUNNING AROUND, YOU MIGHT GET HURT.
NOW WHERE WAS I?
OH YES...
rrrRRRAAH..!
PSST! MALLORY!
YOU CALL THAT TERRORIZING A TOWN? MY MOTHER CAN TERRORIZE BETTER THAN THAT... AND SHE'S OLD!
AND WHAT'S THE BIT WITH THE KID?
SO I GOT A WEAK SPOT FOR KIDS.
SO WHAT?
JUST DO YOUR STUFF AND SAVE THE SNIDE COMMENTS FOR LATER.

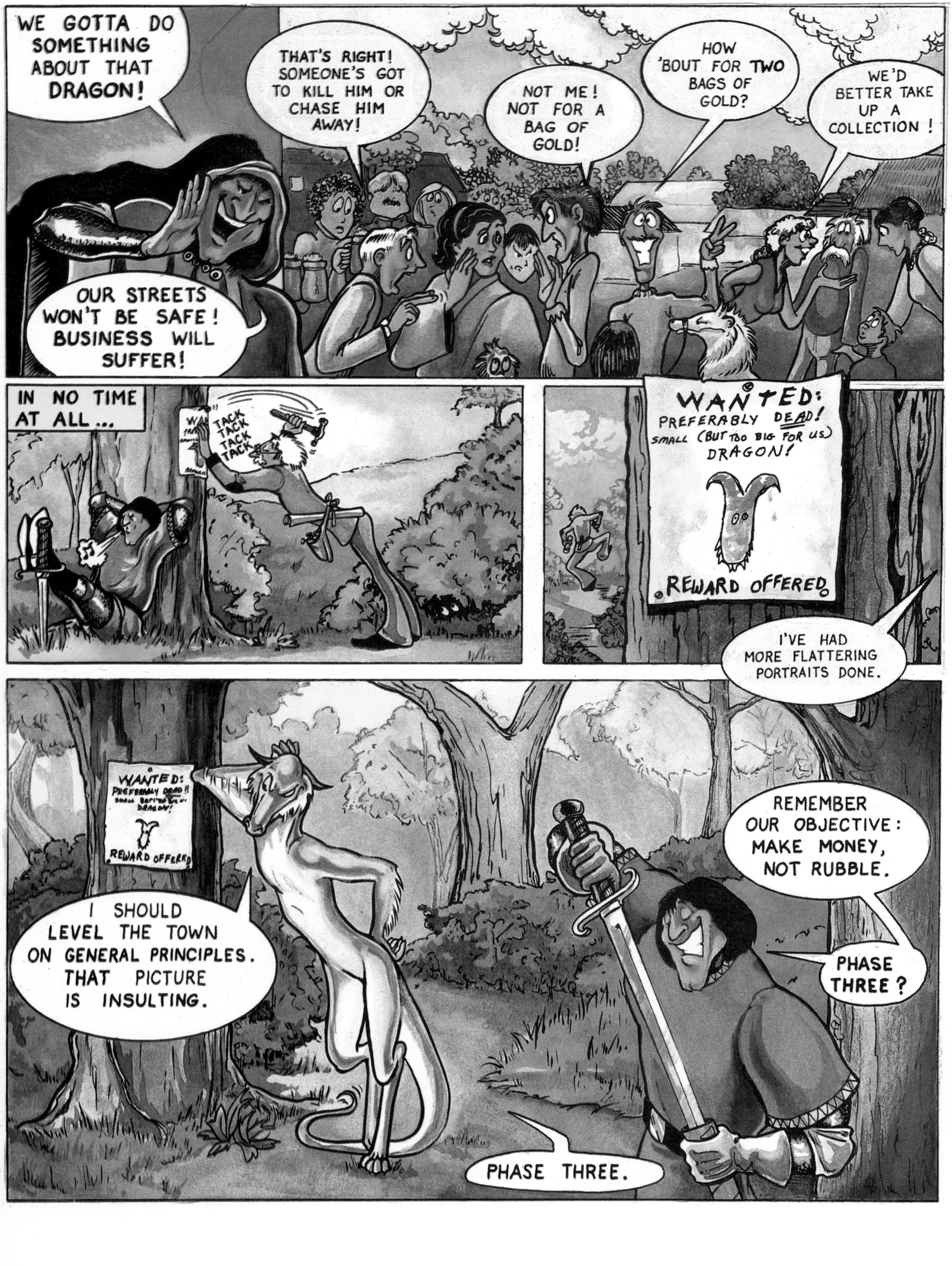
WE GOTTA DO SOMETHING ABOUT THAT DRAGON!
THAT'S RIGHT! SOMEONE'S GOT TO KILL HIM OR CHASE HIM AWAY!
NOT ME! NOT FOR A BAG OF GOLD!
HOW 'BOUT FOR TWO BAGS OF GOLD?
WE'D BETTER TAKE UP A COLLECTION!
OUR STREETS WON'T BE SAFE! BUSINESS WILL SUFFER!
IN NO TIME AT ALL...
TACK TACK TACK TACK
WANTED: PREFERABLY DEAD! SMALL (BUT TOO BIG FOR US) DRAGON!
REWARD OFFERED
I'VE HAD MORE FLATTERING PORTRAITS DONE.
I SHOULD LEVEL THE TOWN ON GENERAL PRINCIPLES. THAT PICTURE IS INSULTING.
REMEMBER OUR OBJECTIVE: MAKE MONEY, NOT RUBBLE.
PHASE THREE?
PHASE THREE.

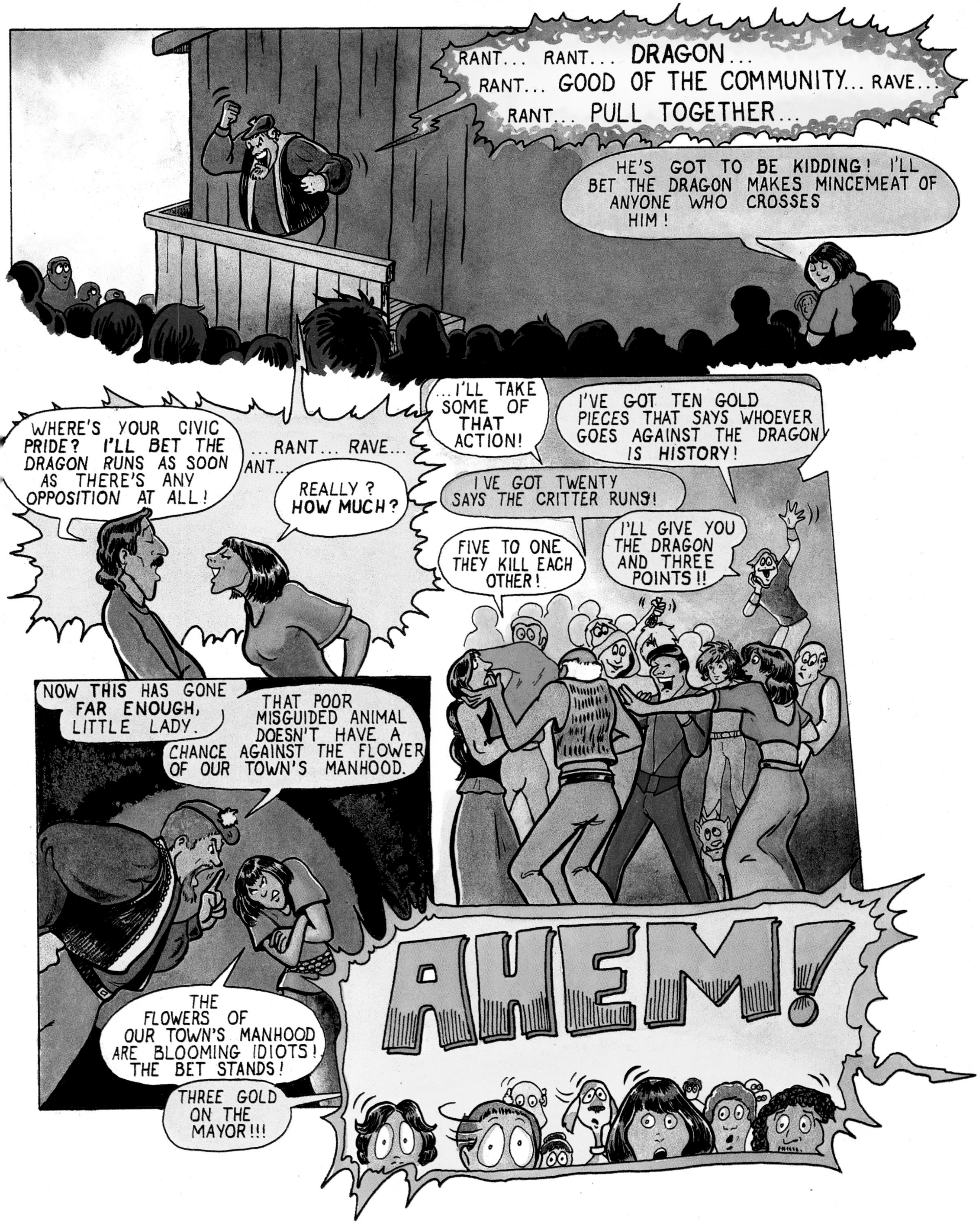
RANT... RANT... DRAGON... RANT... GOOD OF THE COMMUNITY... RAVE... RANT... PULL TOGETHER...
HE'S GOT TO BE KIDDING! I'LL BET THE DRAGON MAKES MINCEMEAT OF ANYONE WHO CROSSES HIM!
WHERE'S YOUR CIVIC PRIDE? I'LL BET THE DRAGON RUNS AS SOON AS THERE'S ANY OPPOSITION AT ALL!
...RANT... RAVE... ANT...
REALLY? HOW MUCH?
...I'LL TAKE SOME OF THAT ACTION!
I'VE GOT TEN GOLD PIECES THAT SAYS WHOEVER GOES AGAINST THE DRAGON IS HISTORY!
I'VE GOT TWENTY SAYS THE CRITTER RUNS!
FIVE TO ONE THEY KILL EACH OTHER!
I'LL GIVE YOU THE DRAGON AND THREE POINTS!!
NOW THIS HAS GONE FAR ENOUGH, LITTLE LADY.
THAT POOR MISGUIDED ANIMAL DOESN'T HAVE A CHANCE AGAINST THE FLOWER OF OUR TOWN'S MANHOOD.
THE FLOWERS OF OUR TOWN'S MANHOOD ARE BLOOMING IDIOTS! THE BET STANDS!
THREE GOLD ON THE MAYOR!!!
AHEM!

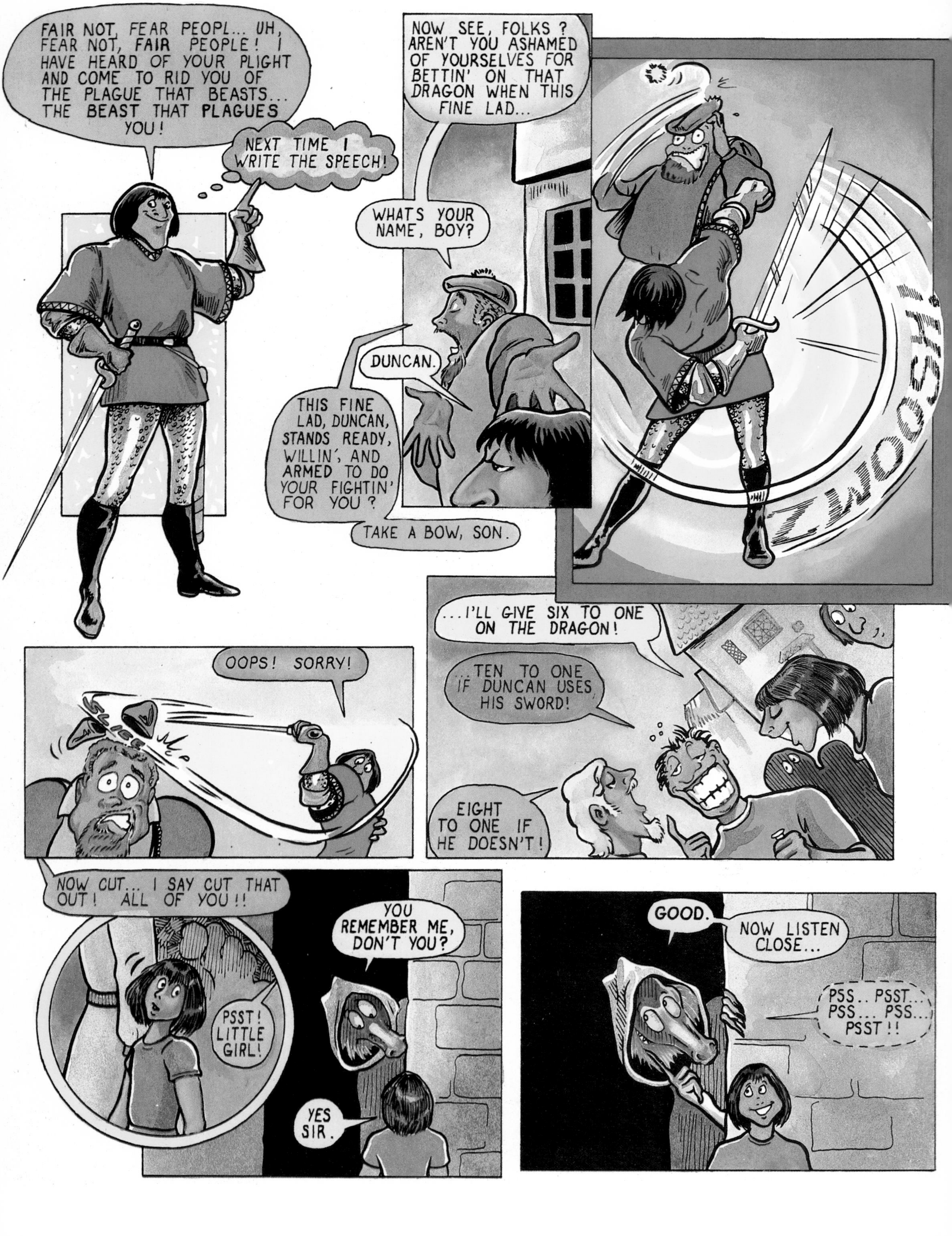
FAIR NOT, FEAR PEOPL... UH, FEAR NOT, FAIR PEOPLE! I HAVE HEARD OF YOUR PLIGHT AND COME TO RID YOU OF THE PLAGUE THAT BEASTS... THE BEAST THAT PLAGUES YOU!
NEXT TIME I WRITE THE SPEECH!
NOW SEE, FOLKS? AREN'T YOU ASHAMED OF YOURSELVES FOR BETTIN' ON THAT DRAGON WHEN THIS FINE LAD...
WHATS YOUR NAME, BOY?
DUNCAN.
THIS FINE LAD, DUNCAN, STANDS READY, WILLIN', AND ARMED TO DO YOUR FIGHTIN' FOR YOU?
TAKE A BOW, SON.
ZWOOOSH!
OOPS! SORRY!
SLICE
...I'LL GIVE SIX TO ONE ON THE DRAGON!
...TEN TO ONE IF DUNCAN USES HIS SWORD!
EIGHT TO ONE IF HE DOESN'T!
NOW CUT... I SAY CUT THAT OUT! ALL OF YOU!!
PSST! LITTLE GIRL!
YOU REMEMBER ME, DON'T YOU?
YES SIR.
GOOD.
NOW LISTEN CLOSE...
PSS.. PSST.. PSS... PSS... PSST!!

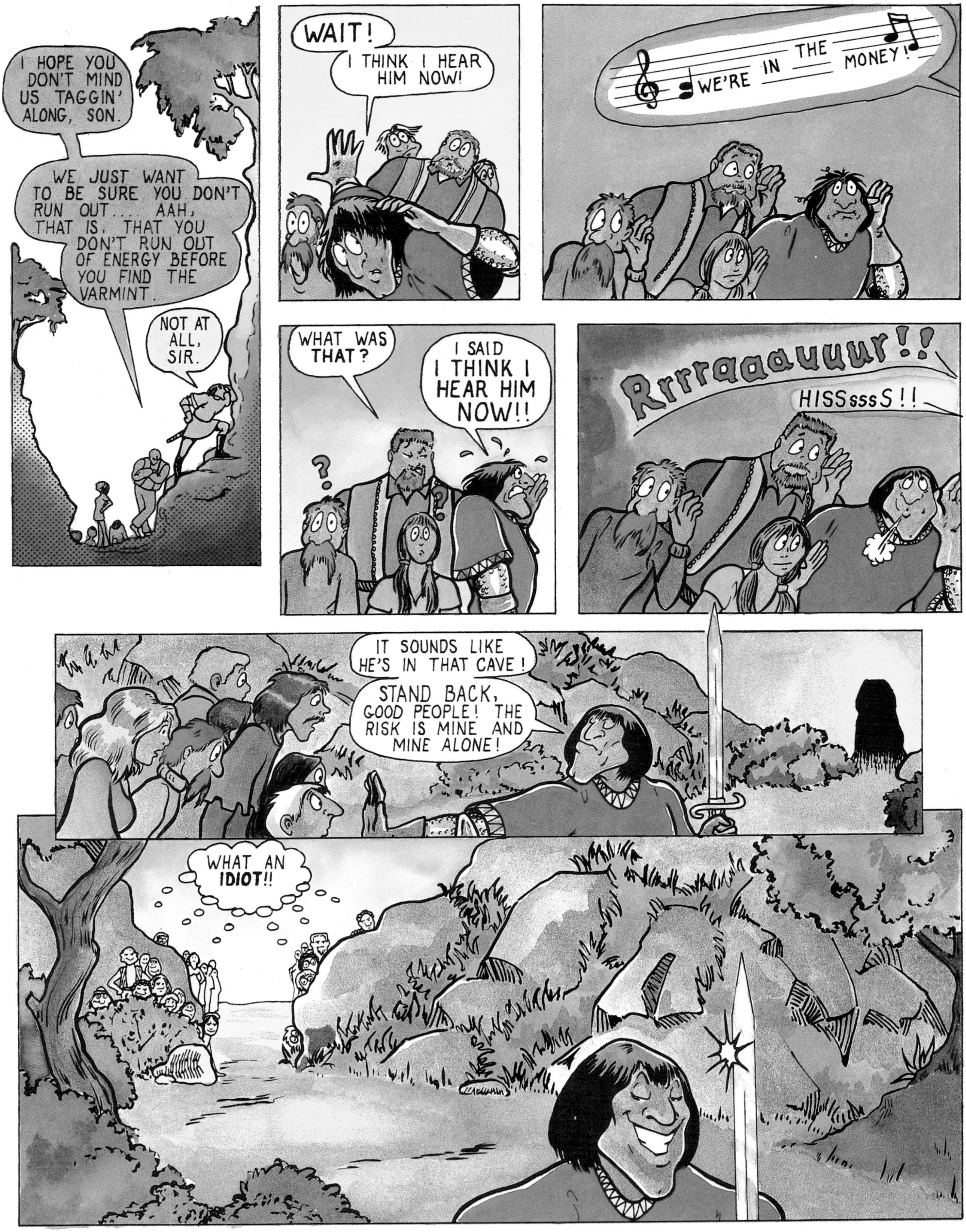
I HOPE YOU DON'T MIND US TAGGIN' ALONG, SON.
WE JUST WANT TO BE SURE YOU DON'T RUN OUT.... AAH, THAT IS, THAT YOU DON'T RUN OUT OF ENERGY BEFORE YOU FIND THE VARMINT.
NOT AT ALL, SIR.
WAIT!
I THINK I HEAR HIM NOW!
WE'RE IN THE MONEY!
WHAT WAS THAT?
I SAID I THINK I HEAR HIM NOW!!
Rrrraaauuur!!
HISSsssS!!
IT SOUNDS LIKE HE'S IN THAT CAVE!
STAND BACK, GOOD PEOPLE! THE RISK IS MINE AND MINE ALONE!
WHAT AN IDIOT!!

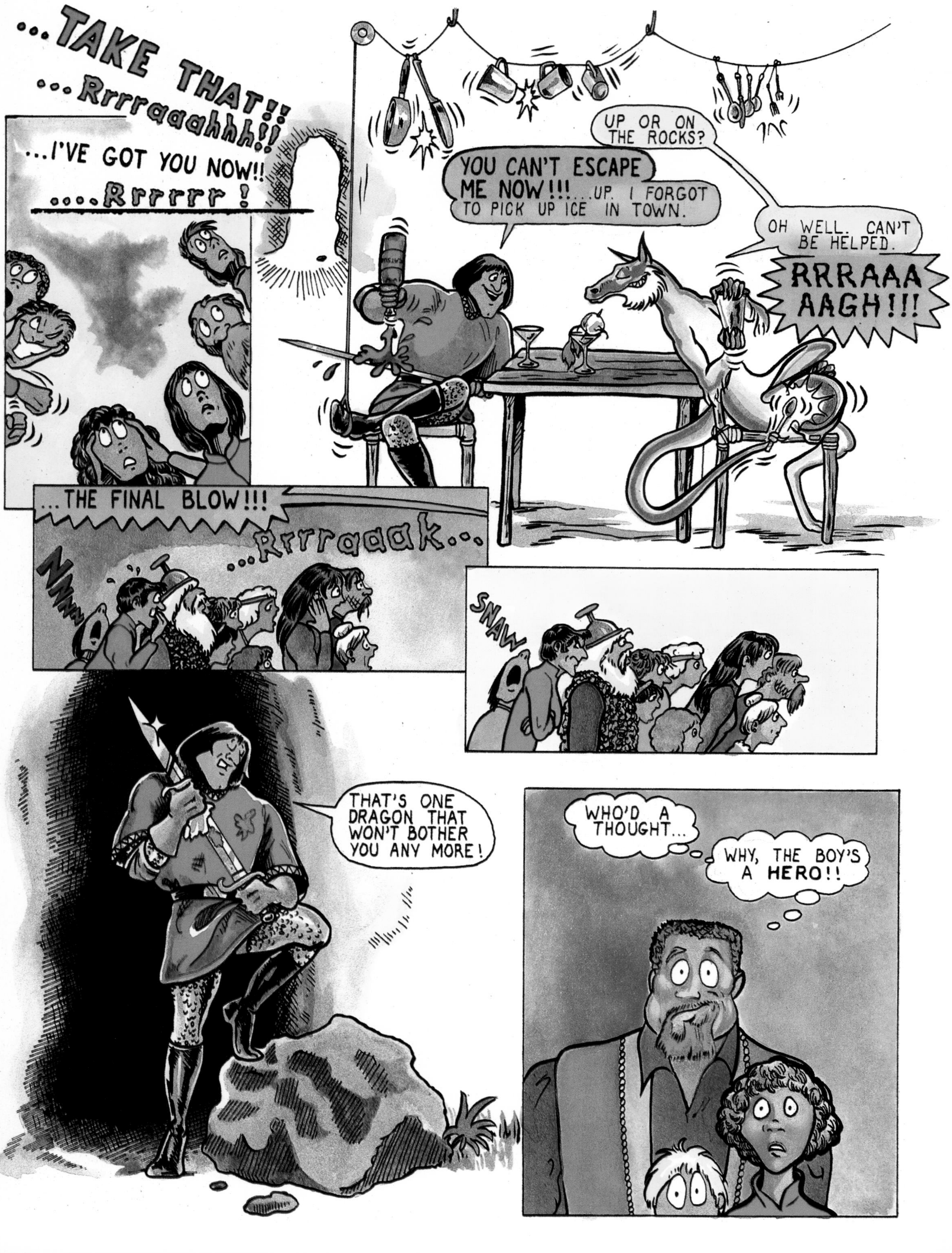

...TAKE THAT!! ...Rrrraaahhh!!
...I'VE GOT YOU NOW!! ....Rrrrrr !
YOU CAN'T ESCAPE ME NOW!!!...UP. I FORGOT TO PICK UP ICE IN TOWN.
UP OR ON THE ROCKS?
OH WELL. CAN'T BE HELPED.
RRRAAA AAGH!!!
...THE FINAL BLOW!!!
...Rrrraaak...
NNNnn
SNAW
THAT'S ONE DRAGON THAT WON'T BOTHER YOU ANY MORE!
WHO'D A THOUGHT...
WHY, THE BOY'S A HERO!!

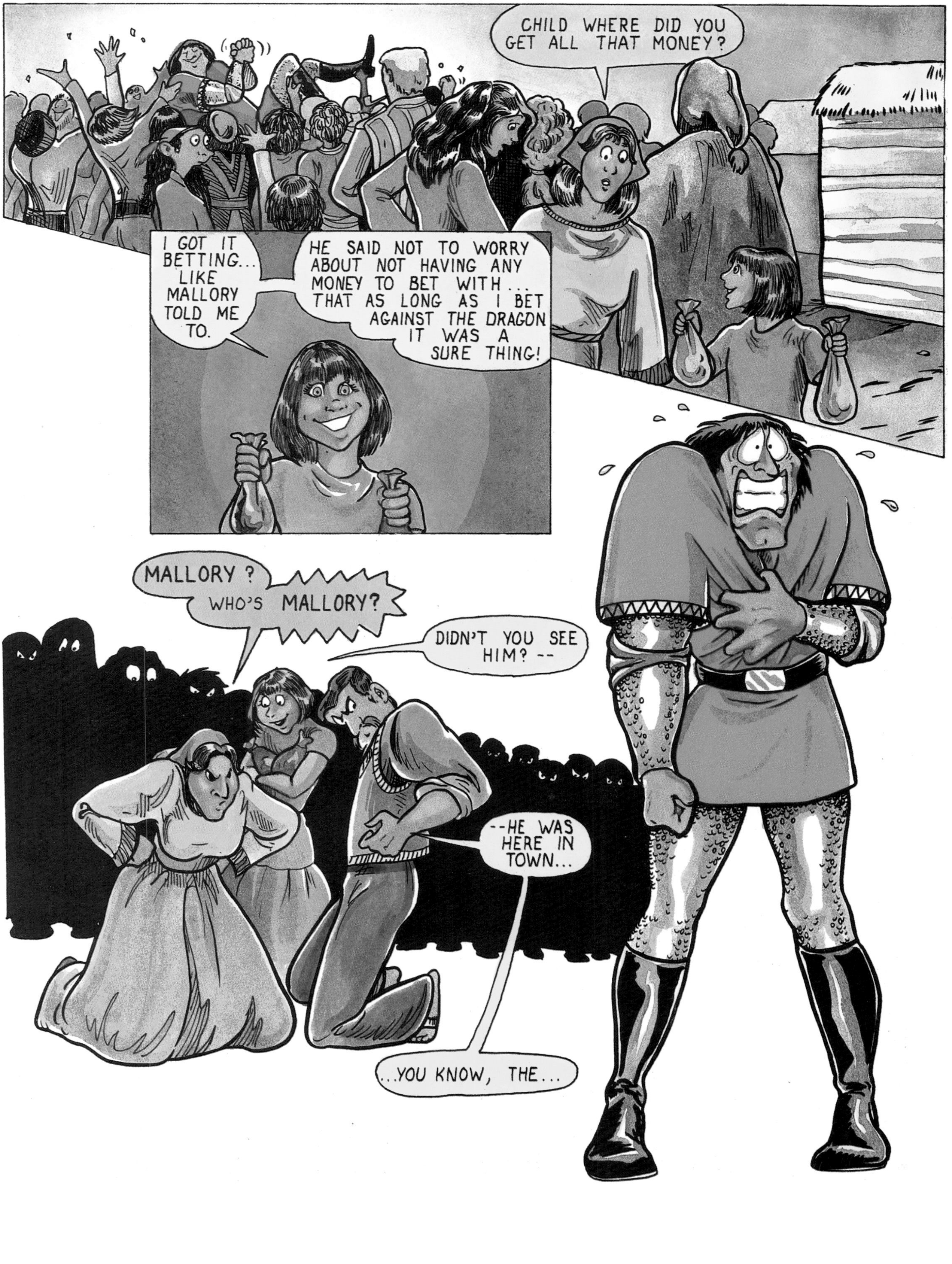
CHILD WHERE DID YOU GET ALL THAT MONEY?
I GOT IT BETTING... LIKE MALLORY TOLD ME TO.
HE SAID NOT TO WORRY ABOUT NOT HAVING ANY MONEY TO BET WITH... THAT AS LONG AS I BET AGAINST THE DRAGON IT WAS A SURE THING!
MALLORY?
WHO'S MALLORY?
DIDN'T YOU SEE HIM? --
--HE WAS HERE IN TOWN...
...YOU KNOW, THE...

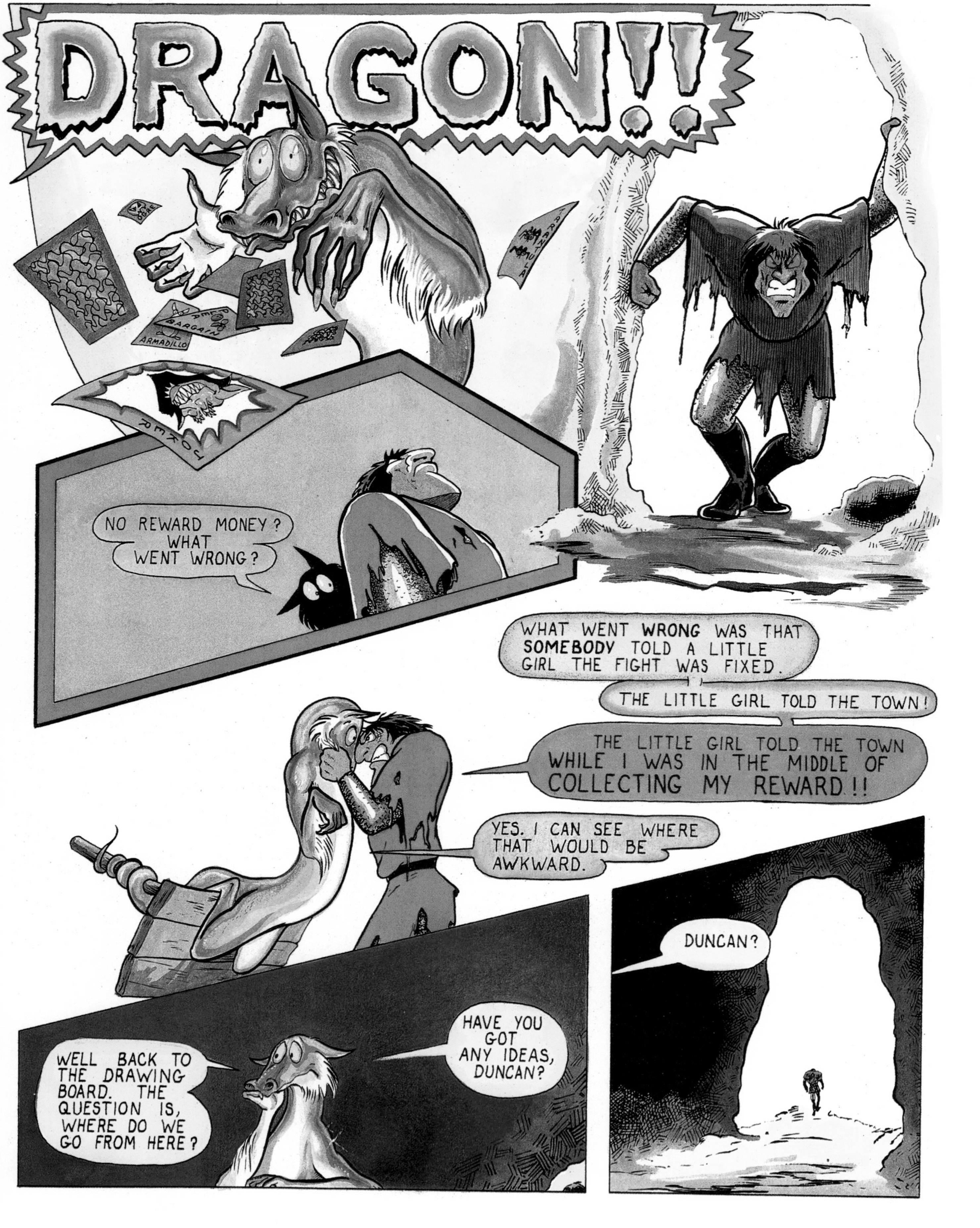
DRAGON!!
NO REWARD MONEY? WHAT WENT WRONG?
WHAT WENT WRONG WAS THAT SOMEBODY TOLD A LITTLE GIRL THE FIGHT WAS FIXED.
THE LITTLE GIRL TOLD THE TOWN!
THE LITTLE GIRL TOLD THE TOWN WHILE I WAS IN THE MIDDLE OF COLLECTING MY REWARD!!
YES. I CAN SEE WHERE THAT WOULD BE AWKWARD.
DUNCAN?
WELL BACK TO THE DRAWING BOARD. THE QUESTION IS, WHERE DO WE GO FROM HERE?
HAVE YOU GOT ANY IDEAS, DUNCAN?

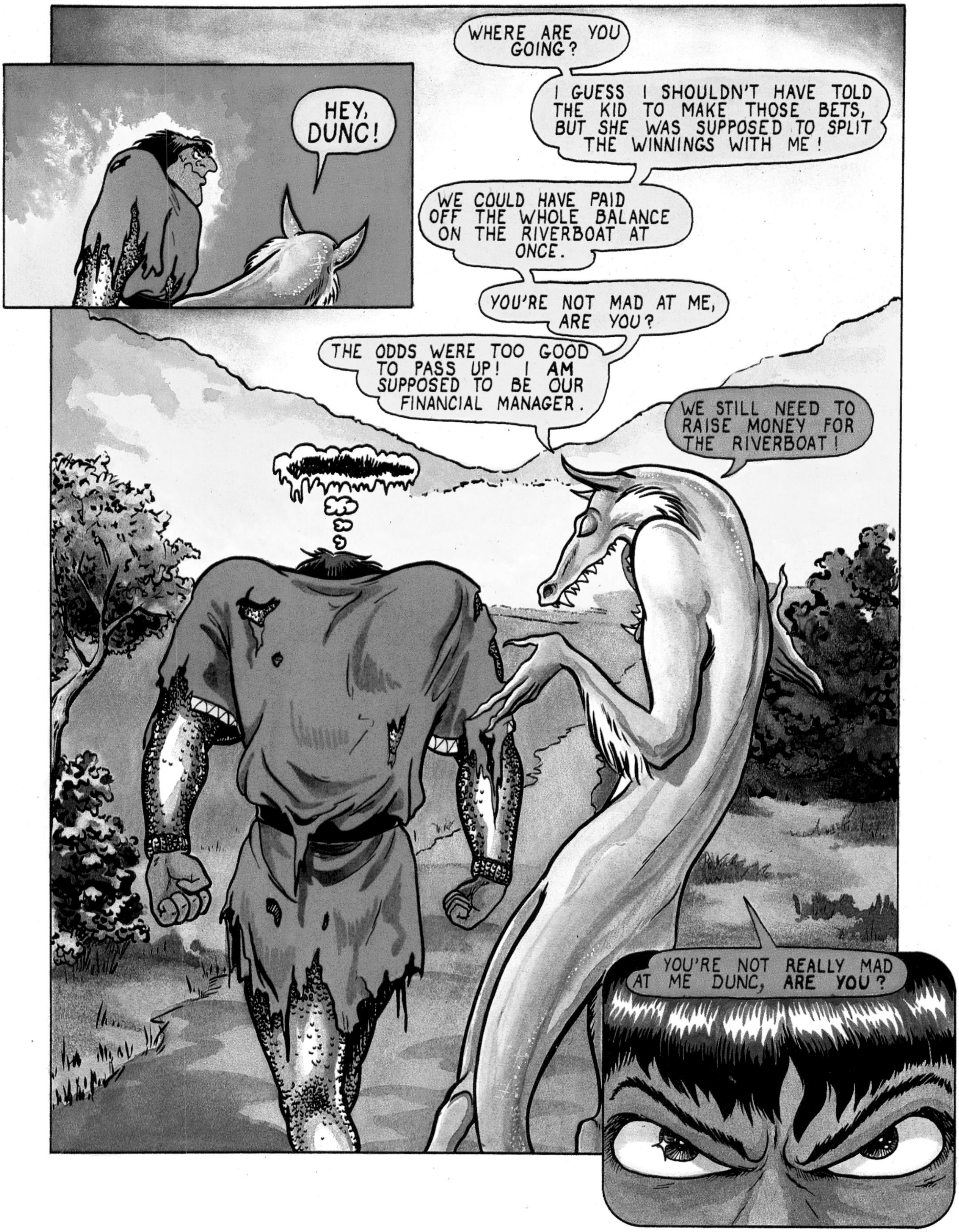
HEY, DUNC!
WHERE ARE YOU GOING?
I GUESS I SHOULDN'T HAVE TOLD THE KID TO MAKE THOSE BETS, BUT SHE WAS SUPPOSED TO SPLIT THE WINNINGS WITH ME!
WE COULD HAVE PAID OFF THE WHOLE BALANCE ON THE RIVERBOAT AT ONCE.
YOU'RE NOT MAD AT ME, ARE YOU?
THE ODDS WERE TOO GOOD TO PASS UP! I AM SUPPOSED TO BE OUR FINANCIAL MANAGER.
WE STILL NEED TO RAISE MONEY FOR THE RIVERBOAT!
YOU'RE NOT REALLY MAD AT ME DUNC, ARE YOU?

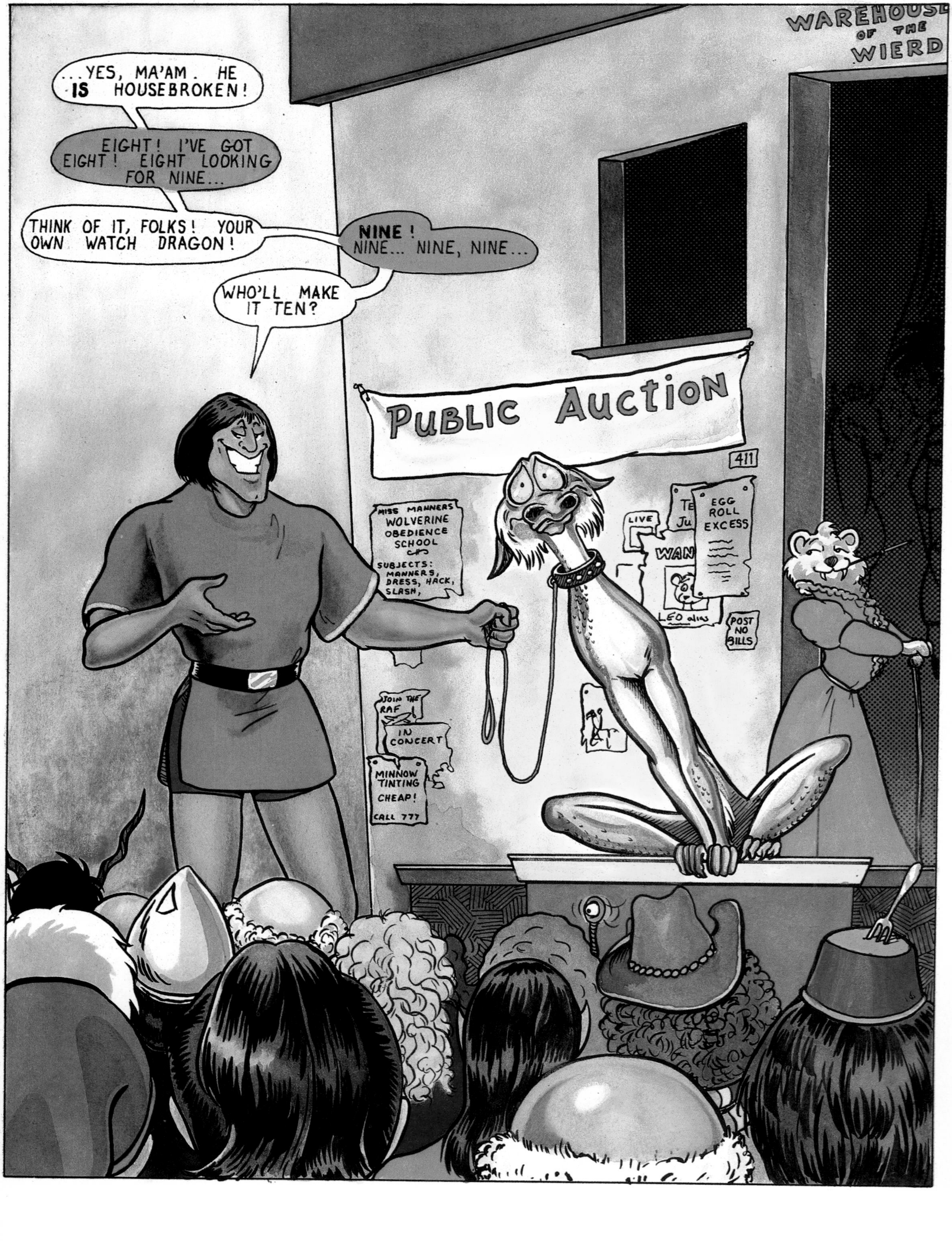

WAREHOUSE OF THE WIERD
...YES, MA'AM. HE IS HOUSEBROKEN!
EIGHT! I'VE GOT EIGHT! EIGHT LOOKING FOR NINE...
THINK OF IT, FOLKS! YOUR OWN WATCH DRAGON!
NINE! NINE... NINE, NINE...
WHO'LL MAKE IT TEN?
PUBLIC AUCTION
411
MISS MANNERS WOLVERINE OBEDIENCE SCHOOL SUBJECTS: MANNERS, DRESS, HACK, SLASH,
EGG ROLL EXCESS
LIVE
POST NO BILLS
JOIN THE RAF
IN CONCERT
MINNOW TINTING CHEAP! CALL 777

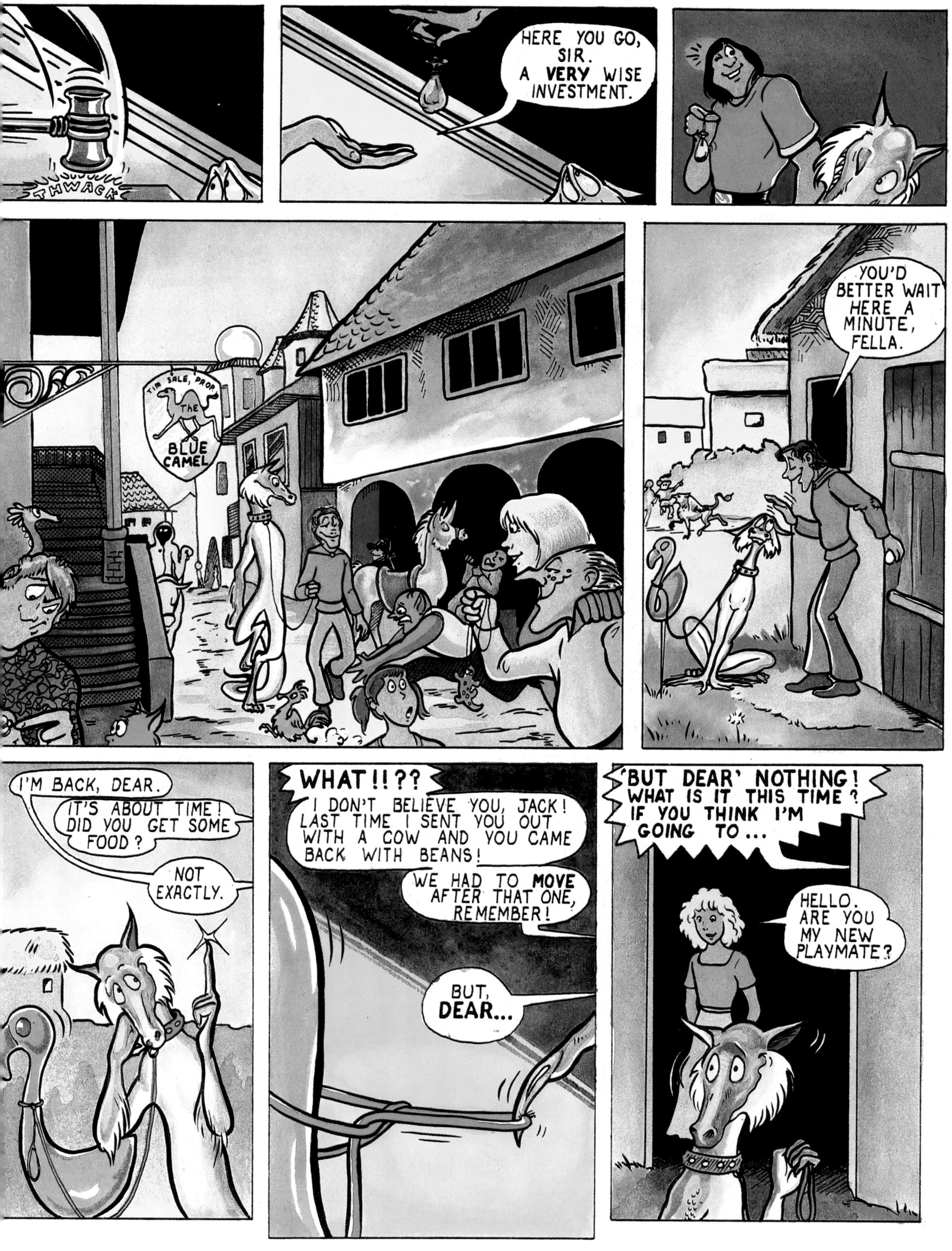
THWACK
HERE YOU GO, SIR. A VERY WISE INVESTMENT.
TIM SALE, PROP. THE BLUE CAMEL
YOU'D BETTER WAIT HERE A MINUTE, FELLA.
I'M BACK, DEAR.
IT'S ABOUT TIME! DID YOU GET SOME FOOD?
NOT EXACTLY.
WHAT!!??
I DON'T BELIEVE YOU, JACK! LAST TIME I SENT YOU OUT WITH A COW AND YOU CAME BACK WITH BEANS!
WE HAD TO MOVE AFTER THAT ONE, REMEMBER!
BUT, DEAR...
'BUT DEAR' NOTHING! WHAT IS IT THIS TIME? IF YOU THINK I'M GOING TO...
HELLO. ARE YOU MY NEW PLAYMATE?

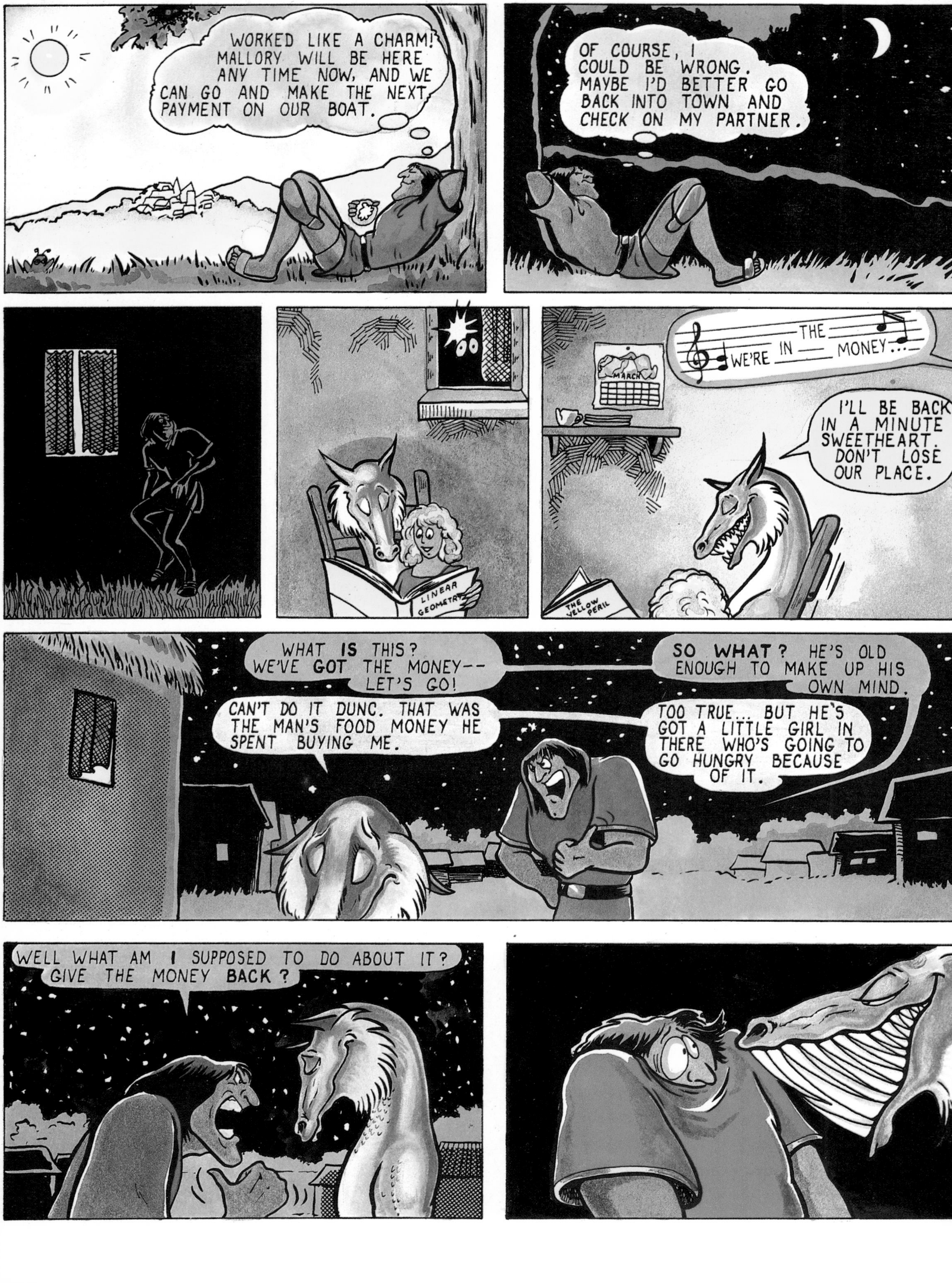
WORKED LIKE A CHARM! MALLORY WILL BE HERE ANY TIME NOW, AND WE CAN GO AND MAKE THE NEXT PAYMENT ON OUR BOAT.
OF COURSE, I COULD BE WRONG. MAYBE I'D BETTER GO BACK INTO TOWN AND CHECK ON MY PARTNER.
LINEAR GEOMETRY
MARCH
WE'RE IN THE MONEY...
I'LL BE BACK IN A MINUTE SWEETHEART. DON'T LOSE OUR PLACE.
THE YELLOW PERIL
WHAT IS THIS? WE'VE GOT THE MONEY-- LET'S GO!
CAN'T DO IT DUNC. THAT WAS THE MAN'S FOOD MONEY HE SPENT BUYING ME.
SO WHAT? HE'S OLD ENOUGH TO MAKE UP HIS OWN MIND.
TOO TRUE... BUT HE'S GOT A LITTLE GIRL IN THERE WHO'S GOING TO GO HUNGRY BECAUSE OF IT.
WELL WHAT AM I SUPPOSED TO DO ABOUT IT? GIVE THE MONEY BACK?

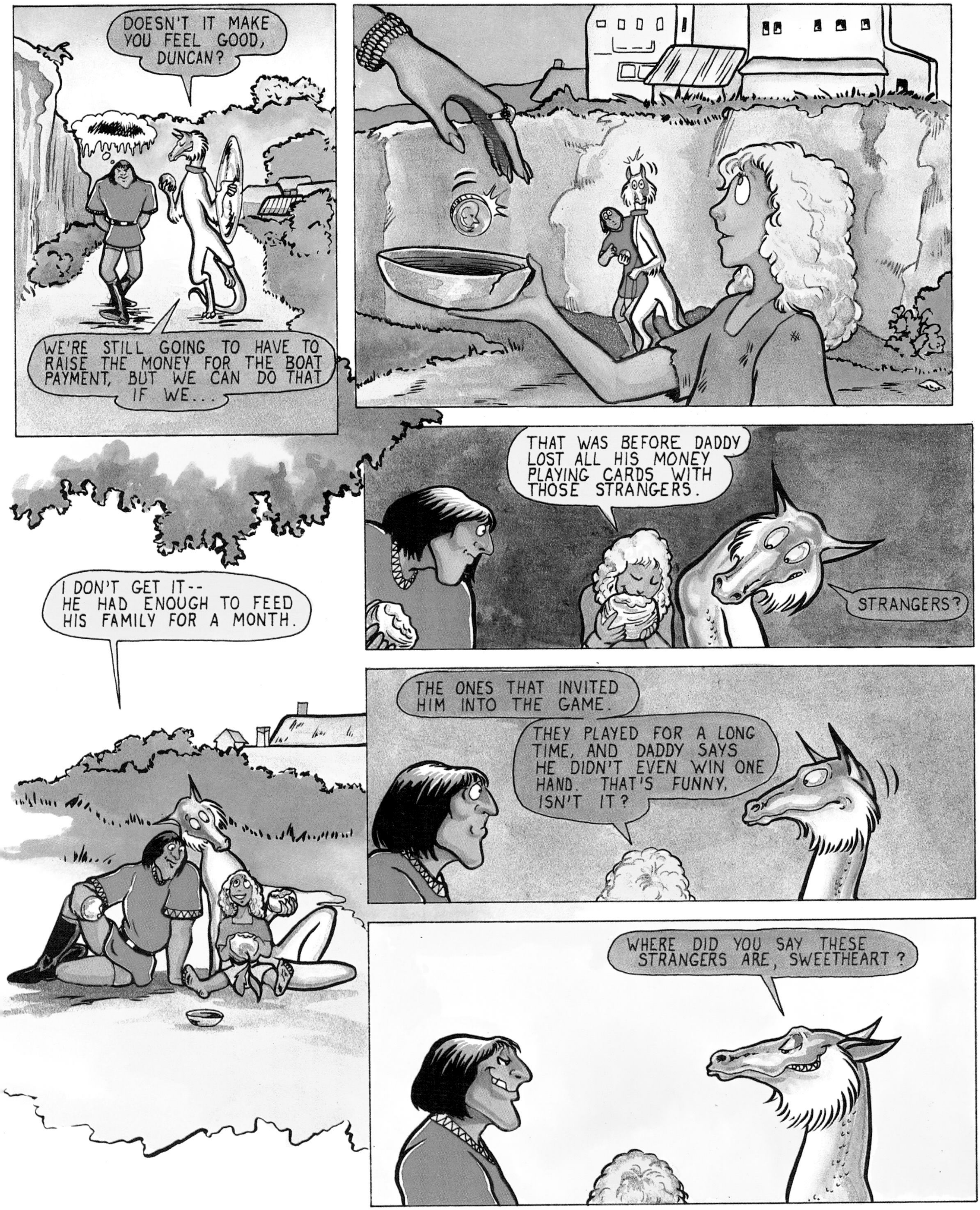
DOESN'T IT MAKE YOU FEEL GOOD, DUNCAN?
WE'RE STILL GOING TO HAVE TO RAISE THE MONEY FOR THE BOAT PAYMENT, BUT WE CAN DO THAT IF WE...
I DON'T GET IT-- HE HAD ENOUGH TO FEED HIS FAMILY FOR A MONTH.
THAT WAS BEFORE DADDY LOST ALL HIS MONEY PLAYING CARDS WITH THOSE STRANGERS.
STRANGERS?
THE ONES THAT INVITED HIM INTO THE GAME.
THEY PLAYED FOR A LONG TIME, AND DADDY SAYS HE DIDN'T EVEN WIN ONE HAND. THAT'S FUNNY, ISN'T IT?
WHERE DID YOU SAY THESE STRANGERS ARE, SWEETHEART?

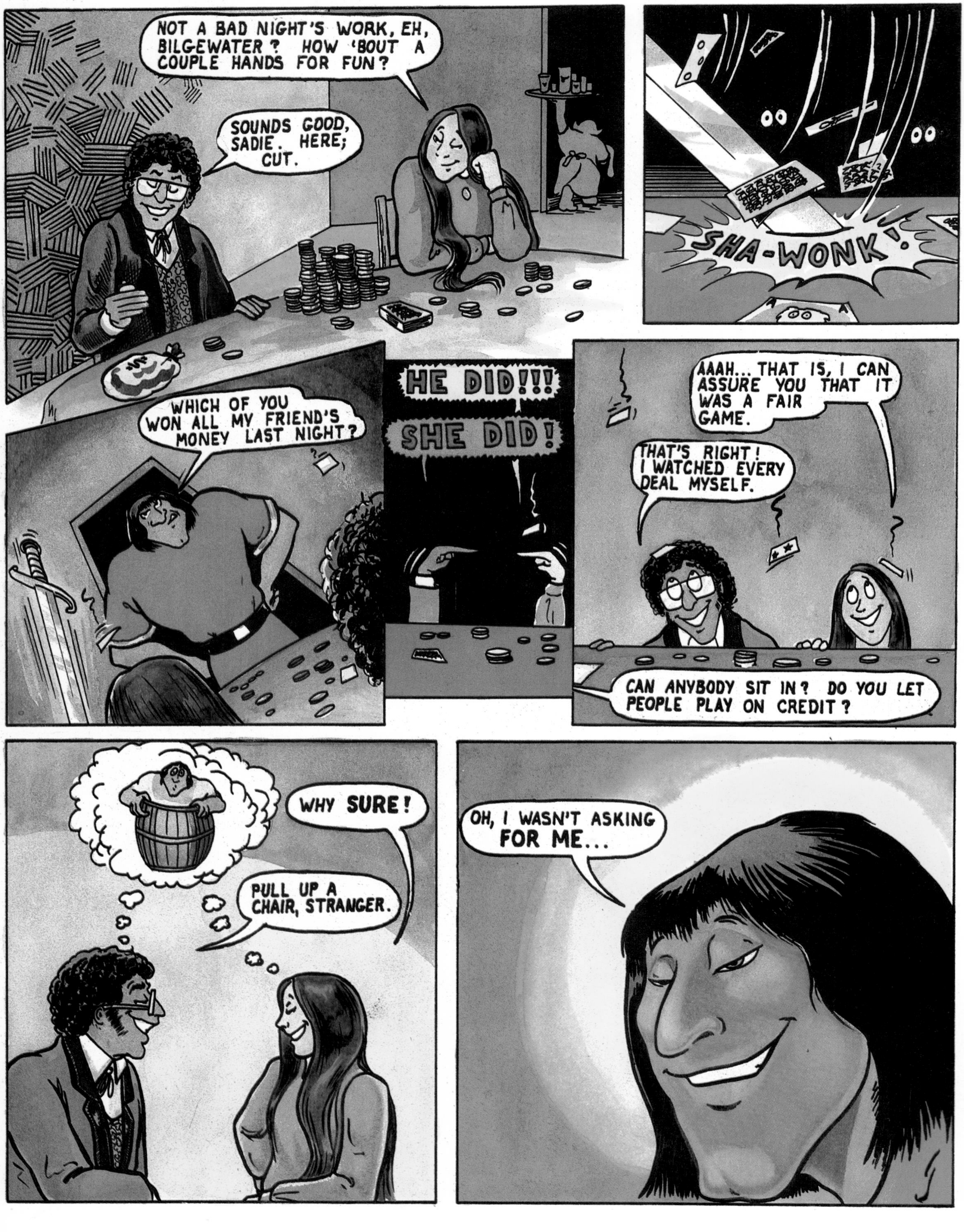

NOT A BAD NIGHT'S WORK, EH, BILGEWATER? HOW 'BOUT A COUPLE HANDS FOR FUN?
SOUNDS GOOD, SADIE. HERE; CUT.
SHA-WONK!
WHICH OF YOU WON ALL MY FRIEND'S MONEY LAST NIGHT?
HE DID!!!
SHE DID!
AAAH... THAT IS, I CAN ASSURE YOU THAT IT WAS A FAIR GAME.
THAT'S RIGHT! I WATCHED EVERY DEAL MYSELF.
CAN ANYBODY SIT IN? DO YOU LET PEOPLE PLAY ON CREDIT?
WHY SURE!
PULL UP A CHAIR, STRANGER.
OH, I WASN'T ASKING FOR ME...

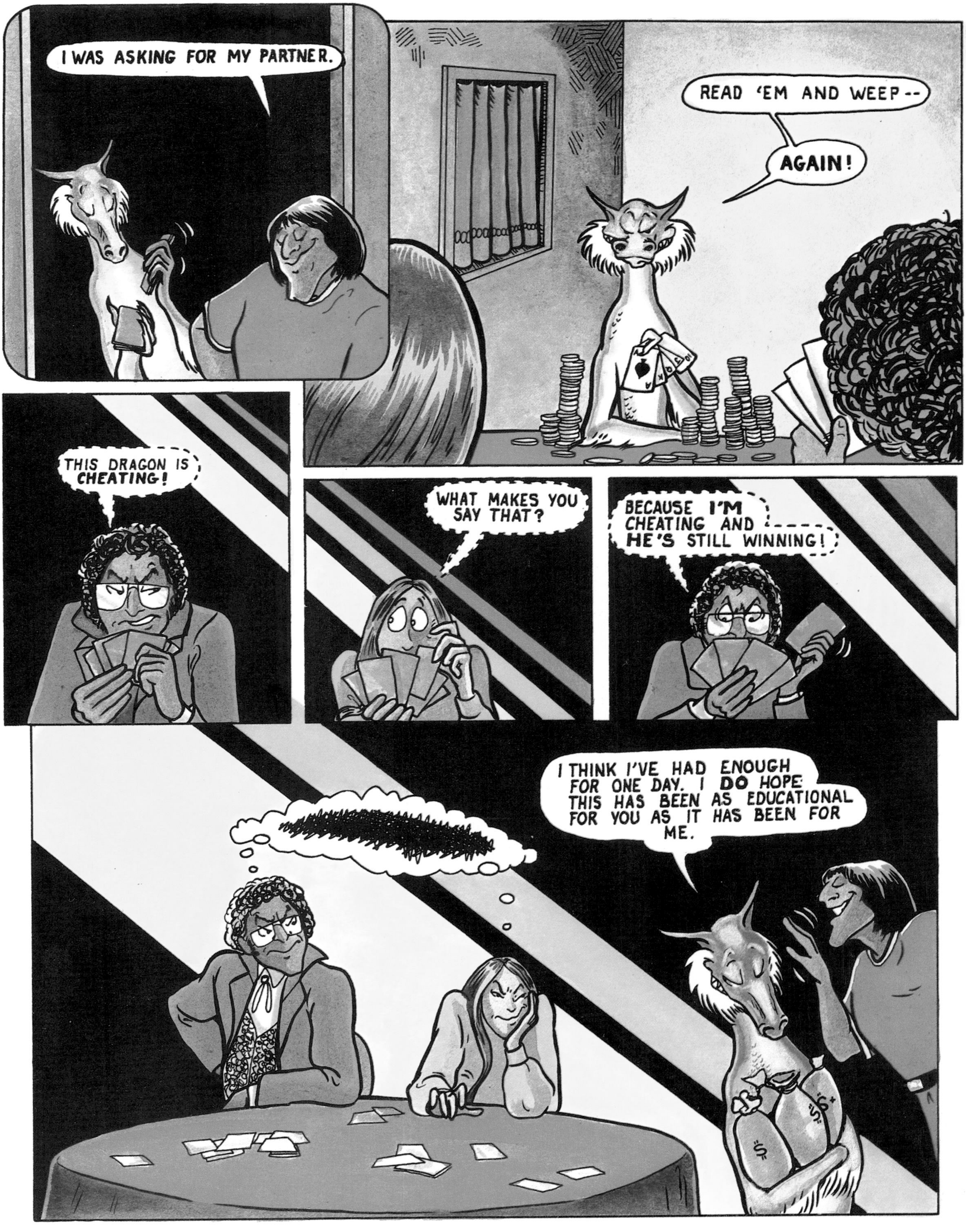
I WAS ASKING FOR MY PARTNER.
READ 'EM AND WEEP --
AGAIN!
THIS DRAGON IS CHEATING!
WHAT MAKES YOU SAY THAT?
BECAUSE I'M CHEATING AND HE'S STILL WINNING!
I THINK I'VE HAD ENOUGH FOR ONE DAY. I DO HOPE THIS HAS BEEN AS EDUCATIONAL FOR YOU AS IT HAS BEEN FOR ME.

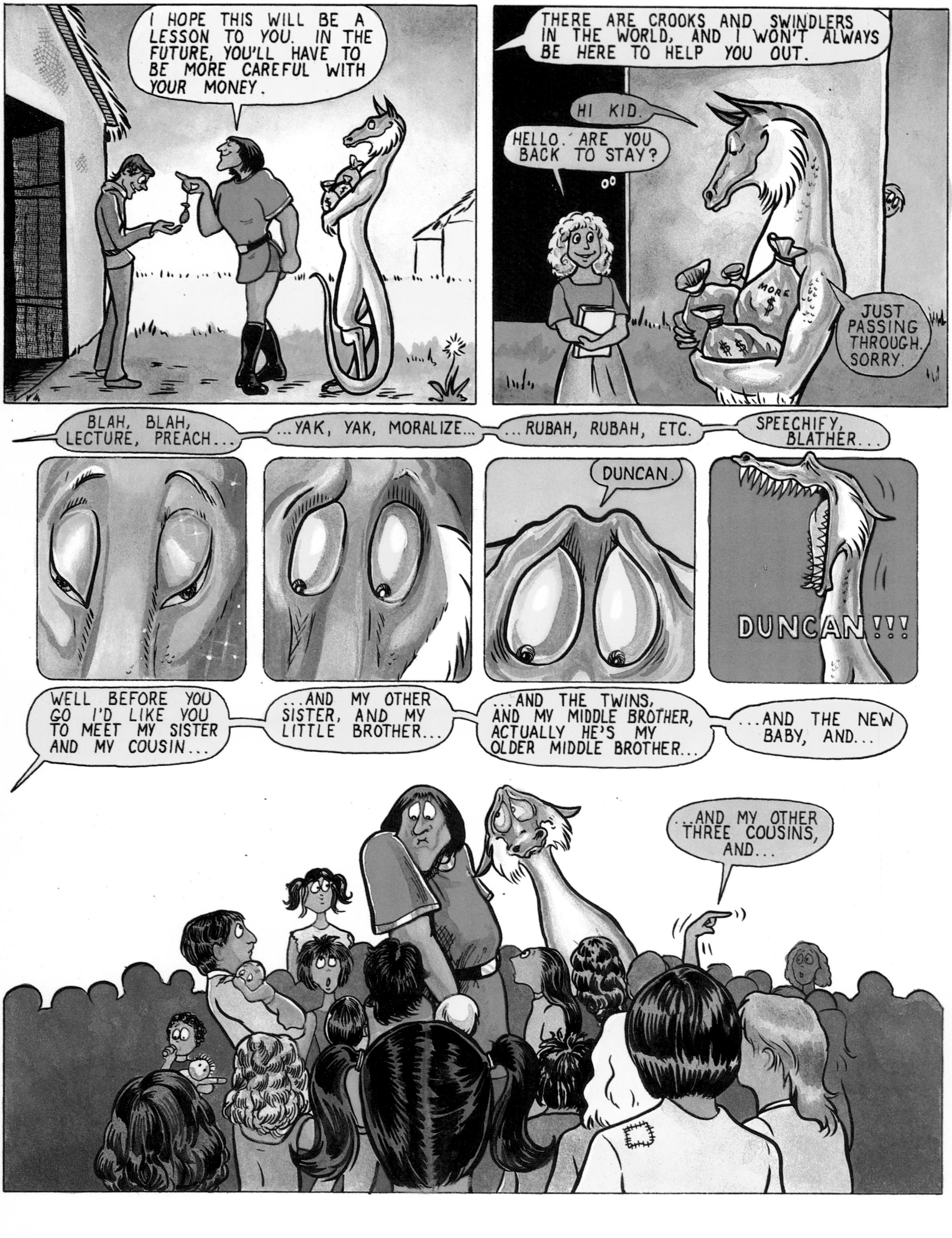
I HOPE THIS WILL BE A LESSON TO YOU. IN THE FUTURE, YOU'LL HAVE TO BE MORE CAREFUL WITH YOUR MONEY.
THERE ARE CROOKS AND SWINDLERS IN THE WORLD, AND I WON'T ALWAYS BE HERE TO HELP YOU OUT.
HI KID.
HELLO. ARE YOU BACK TO STAY?
JUST PASSING THROUGH. SORRY.
MORE $
$ $
BLAH, BLAH, LECTURE, PREACH...
...YAK, YAK, MORALIZE...
...RUBAH, RUBAH, ETC.
SPEECHIFY, BLATHER...
DUNCAN.
DUNCAN!!!
WELL BEFORE YOU GO I'D LIKE YOU TO MEET MY SISTER AND MY COUSIN...
...AND MY OTHER SISTER, AND MY LITTLE BROTHER...
...AND THE TWINS, AND MY MIDDLE BROTHER, ACTUALLY HE'S MY OLDER MIDDLE BROTHER...
...AND THE NEW BABY, AND...
...AND MY OTHER THREE COUSINS, AND...

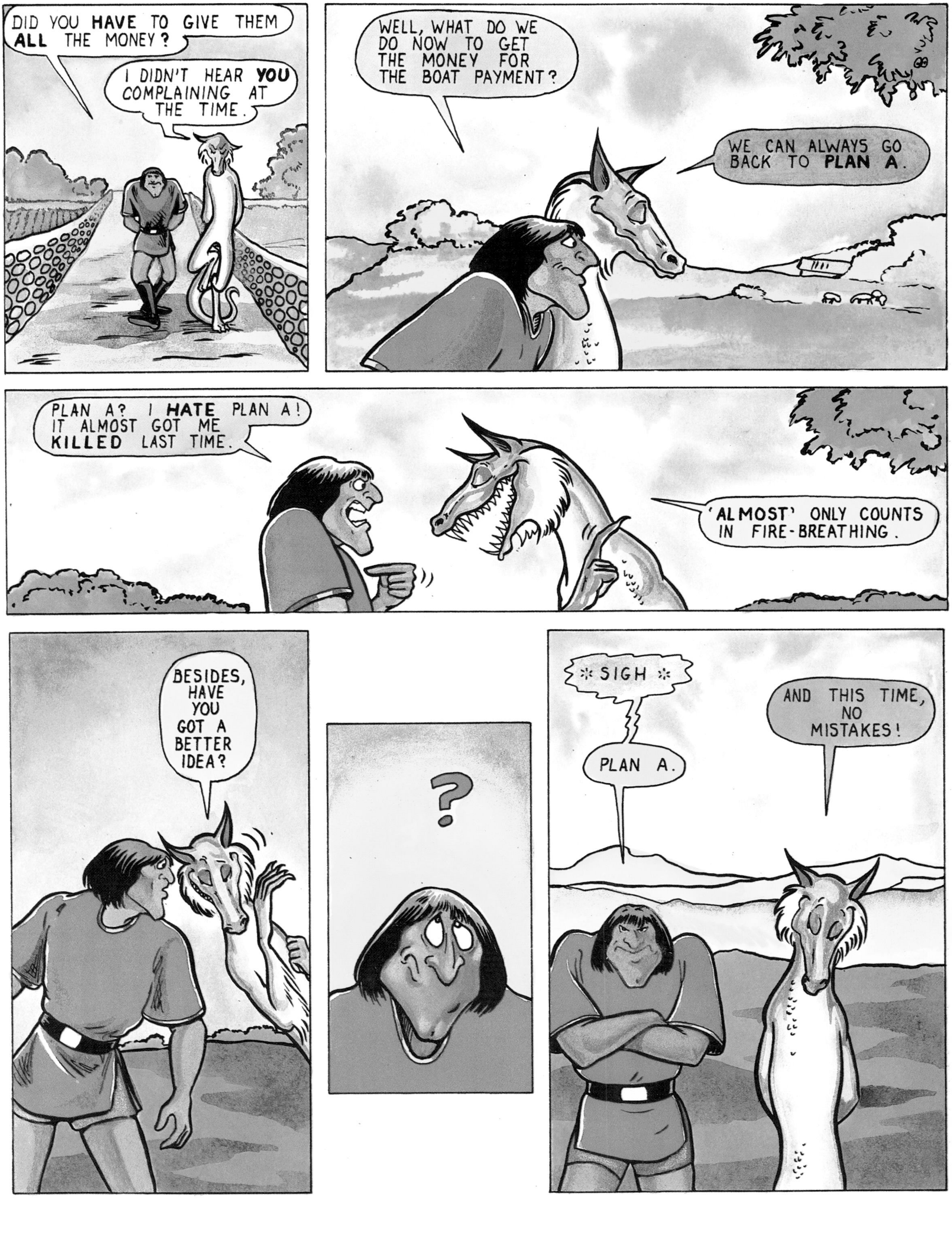
DID YOU HAVE TO GIVE THEM ALL THE MONEY?
I DIDN'T HEAR YOU COMPLAINING AT THE TIME.
WELL, WHAT DO WE DO NOW TO GET THE MONEY FOR THE BOAT PAYMENT?
WE CAN ALWAYS GO BACK TO PLAN A.
PLAN A? I HATE PLAN A! IT ALMOST GOT ME KILLED LAST TIME.
'ALMOST' ONLY COUNTS IN FIRE-BREATHING.
BESIDES, HAVE YOU GOT A BETTER IDEA?
?
* SIGH *
PLAN A.
AND THIS TIME, NO MISTAKES!

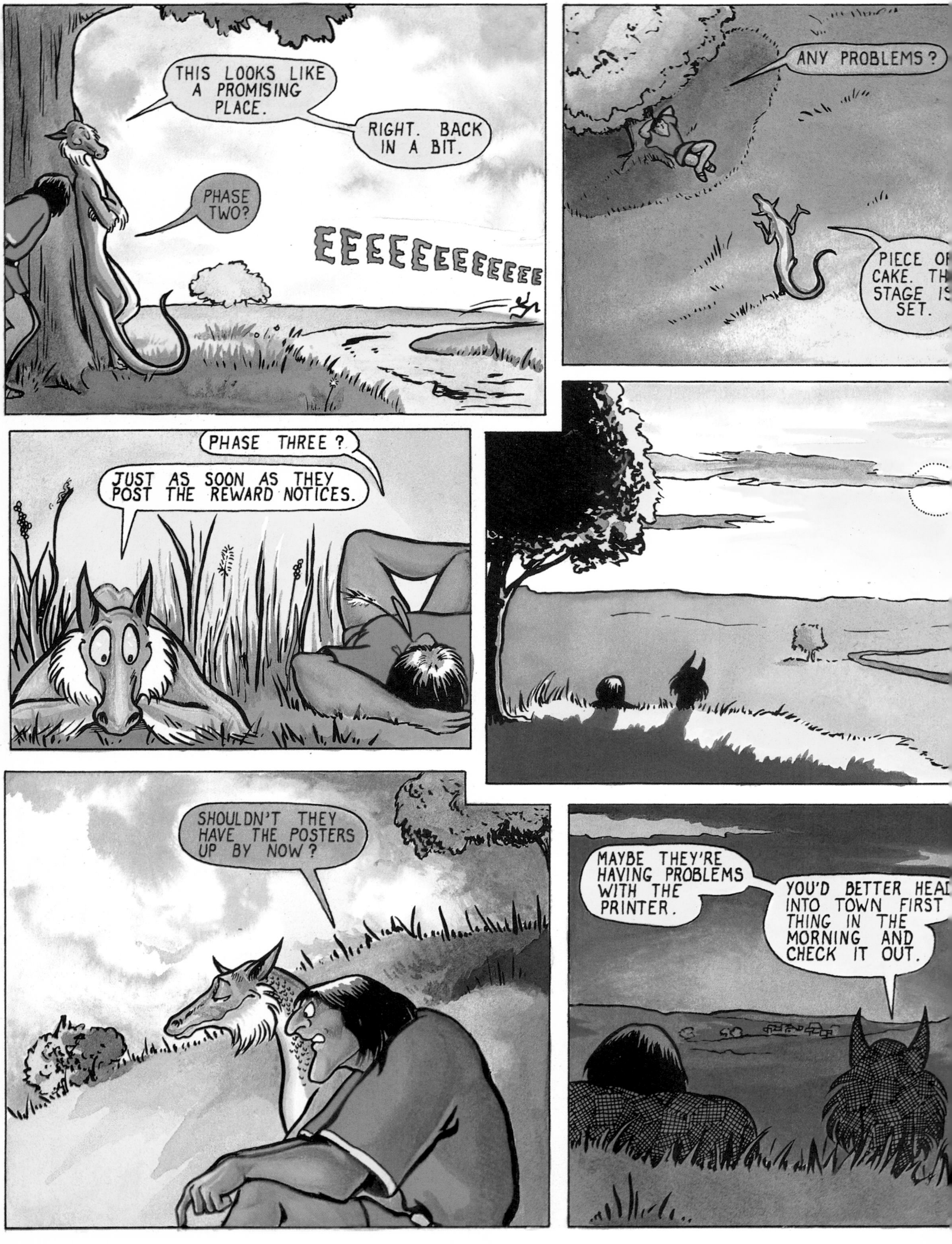
THIS LOOKS LIKE A PROMISING PLACE.
RIGHT. BACK IN A BIT.
PHASE TWO?
EEEEEEEEEEEEE
ANY PROBLEMS?
PIECE OF CAKE. TH STAGE IS SET.
PHASE THREE?
JUST AS SOON AS THEY POST THE REWARD NOTICES.
SHOULDN'T THEY HAVE THE POSTERS UP BY NOW?
MAYBE THEY'RE HAVING PROBLEMS WITH THE PRINTER.
YOU'D BETTER HEAD INTO TOWN FIRST THING IN THE MORNING AND CHECK IT OUT.

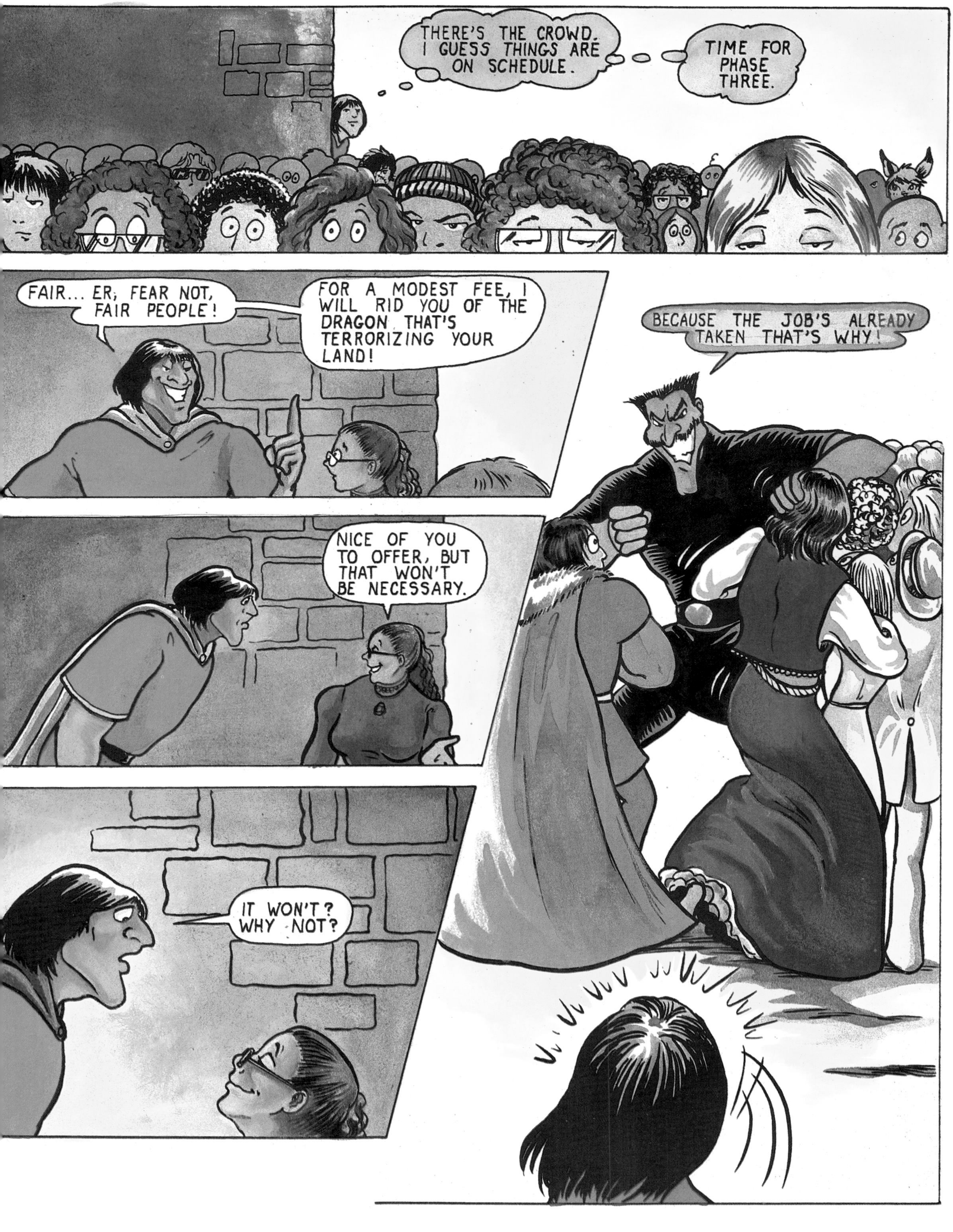
THERE'S THE CROWD. I GUESS THINGS ARE ON SCHEDULE.
TIME FOR PHASE THREE.
FAIR... ER; FEAR NOT, FAIR PEOPLE!
FOR A MODEST FEE, I WILL RID YOU OF THE DRAGON THAT'S TERRORIZING YOUR LAND!
NICE OF YOU TO OFFER, BUT THAT WON'T BE NECESSARY.
IT WON'T? WHY NOT?
BECAUSE THE JOB'S ALREADY TAKEN THAT'S WHY!

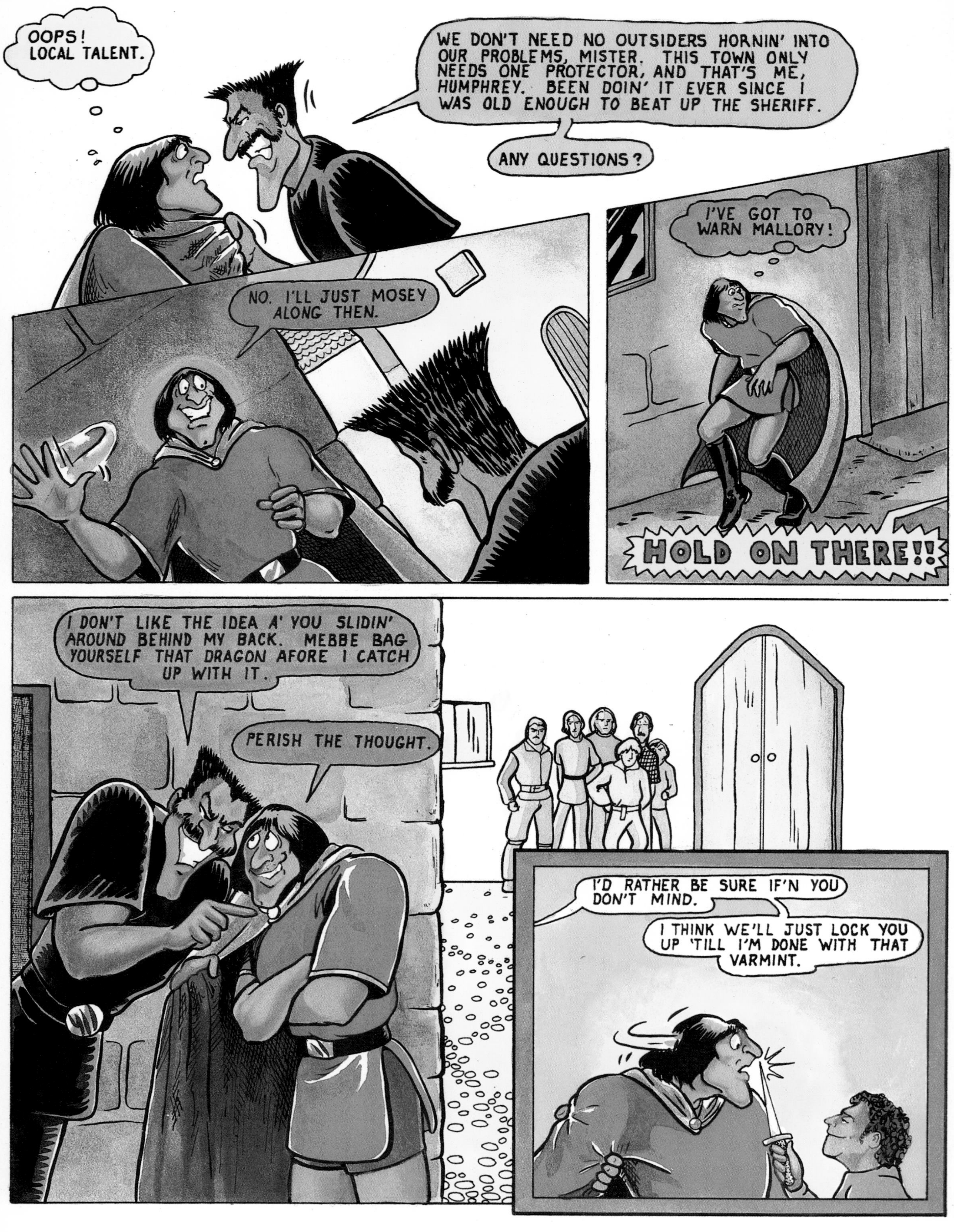
OOPS! LOCAL TALENT.
WE DON'T NEED NO OUTSIDERS HORNIN' INTO OUR PROBLEMS, MISTER. THIS TOWN ONLY NEEDS ONE PROTECTOR, AND THAT'S ME, HUMPHREY. BEEN DOIN' IT EVER SINCE I WAS OLD ENOUGH TO BEAT UP THE SHERIFF.
ANY QUESTIONS?
NO. I'LL JUST MOSEY ALONG THEN.
I'VE GOT TO WARN MALLORY!
HOLD ON THERE!!
I DON'T LIKE THE IDEA A' YOU SLIDIN' AROUND BEHIND MY BACK. MEBBE BAG YOURSELF THAT DRAGON AFORE I CATCH UP WITH IT.
PERISH THE THOUGHT.
I'D RATHER BE SURE IF'N YOU DON'T MIND.
I THINK WE'LL JUST LOCK YOU UP 'TILL I'M DONE WITH THAT VARMINT.

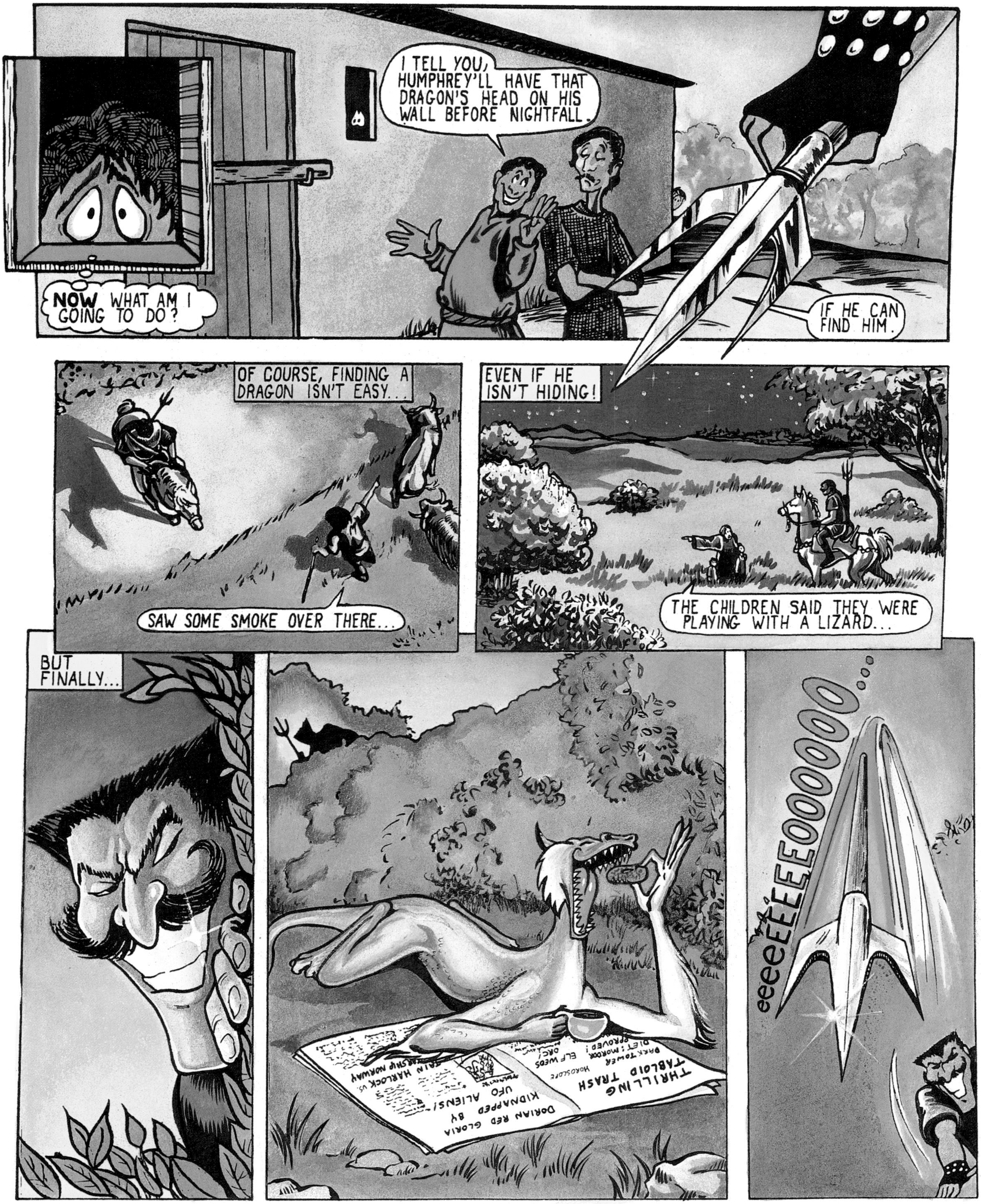
I TELL YOU, HUMPHREY'LL HAVE THAT DRAGON'S HEAD ON HIS WALL BEFORE NIGHTFALL.
IF HE CAN FIND HIM.
NOW WHAT AM I GOING TO DO?
OF COURSE, FINDING A DRAGON ISN'T EASY...
SAW SOME SMOKE OVER THERE...
EVEN IF HE ISN'T HIDING!
THE CHILDREN SAID THEY WERE PLAYING WITH A LIZARD...
BUT FINALLY...
THRILLING TABLOID TRASH
HOROSCOPE
DORIAN RED GLORIA KIDNAPPED BY UFO ALIENS!
eeeeEEEEEOOOOOOO...

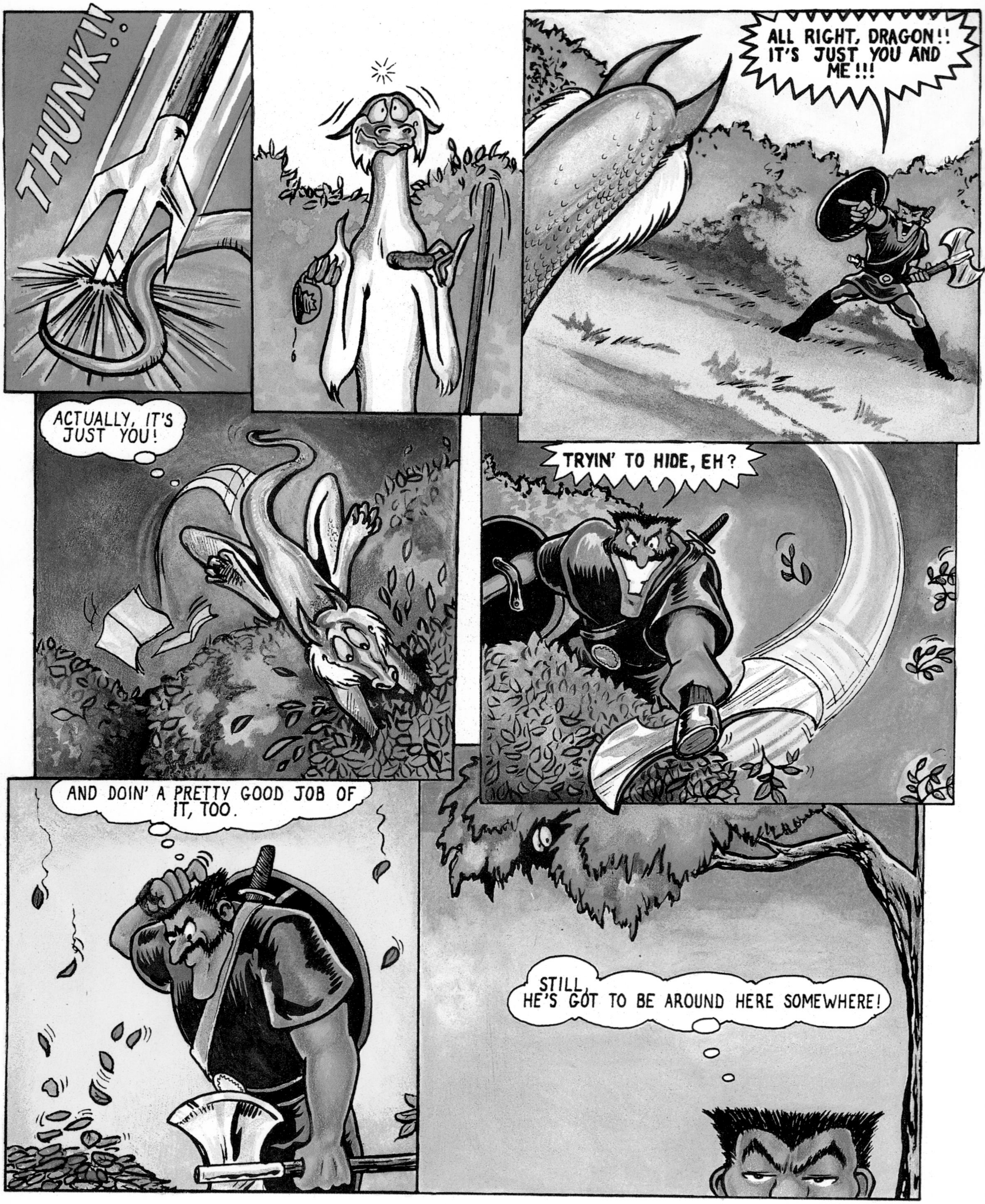
THUNK!!
ALL RIGHT, DRAGON!! IT'S JUST YOU AND ME!!!
ACTUALLY, IT'S JUST YOU!
TRYIN' TO HIDE, EH?
AND DOIN' A PRETTY GOOD JOB OF IT, TOO.
STILL, HE'S GOT TO BE AROUND HERE SOMEWHERE!

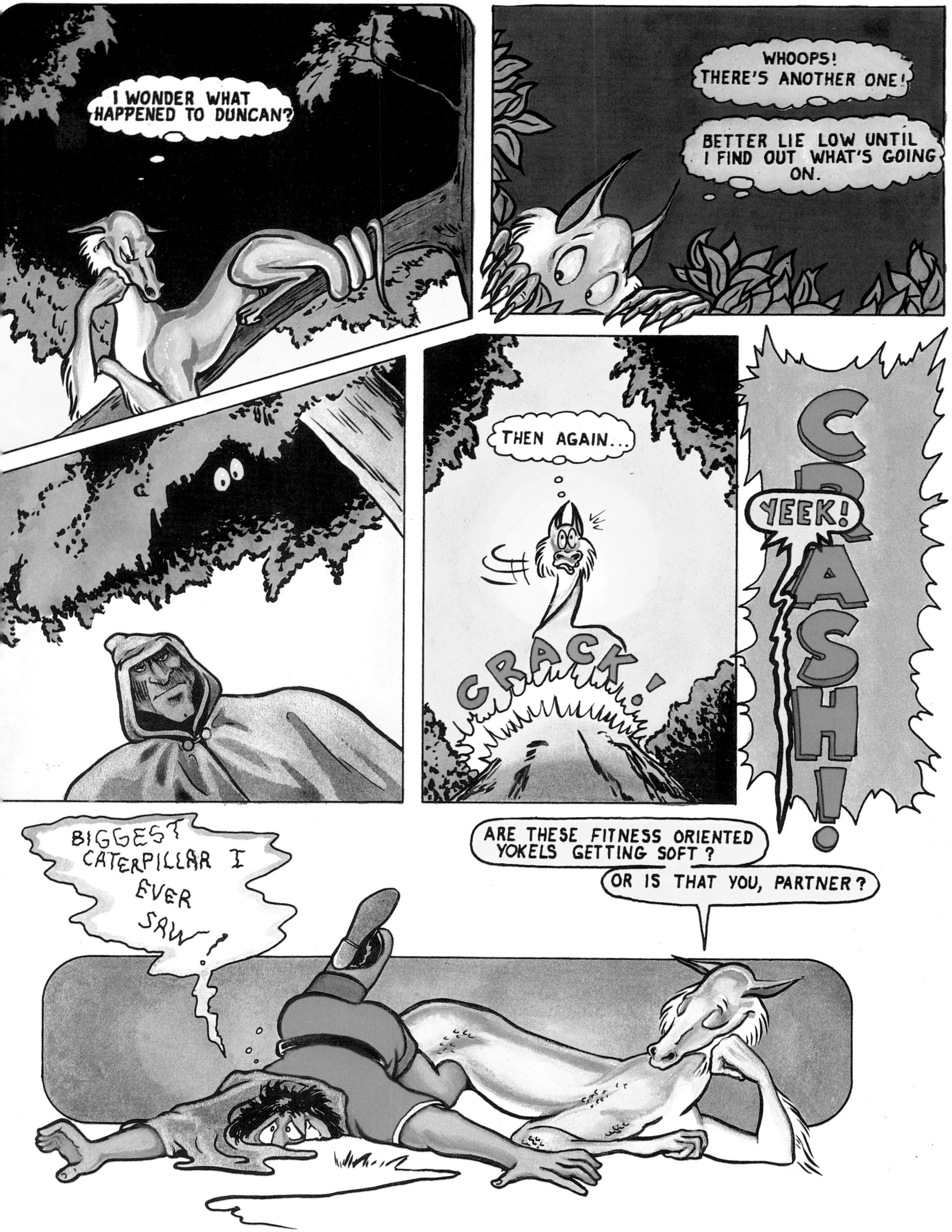

I WONDER WHAT HAPPENED TO DUNCAN?
WHOOPS! THERE'S ANOTHER ONE!
BETTER LIE LOW UNTIL I FIND OUT WHAT'S GOING ON.
THEN AGAIN...
CRACK!
CRASH!
YEEK!
BIGGEST CATERPILLAR I EVER SAW!
ARE THESE FITNESS ORIENTED YOKELS GETTING SOFT?
OR IS THAT YOU, PARTNER?

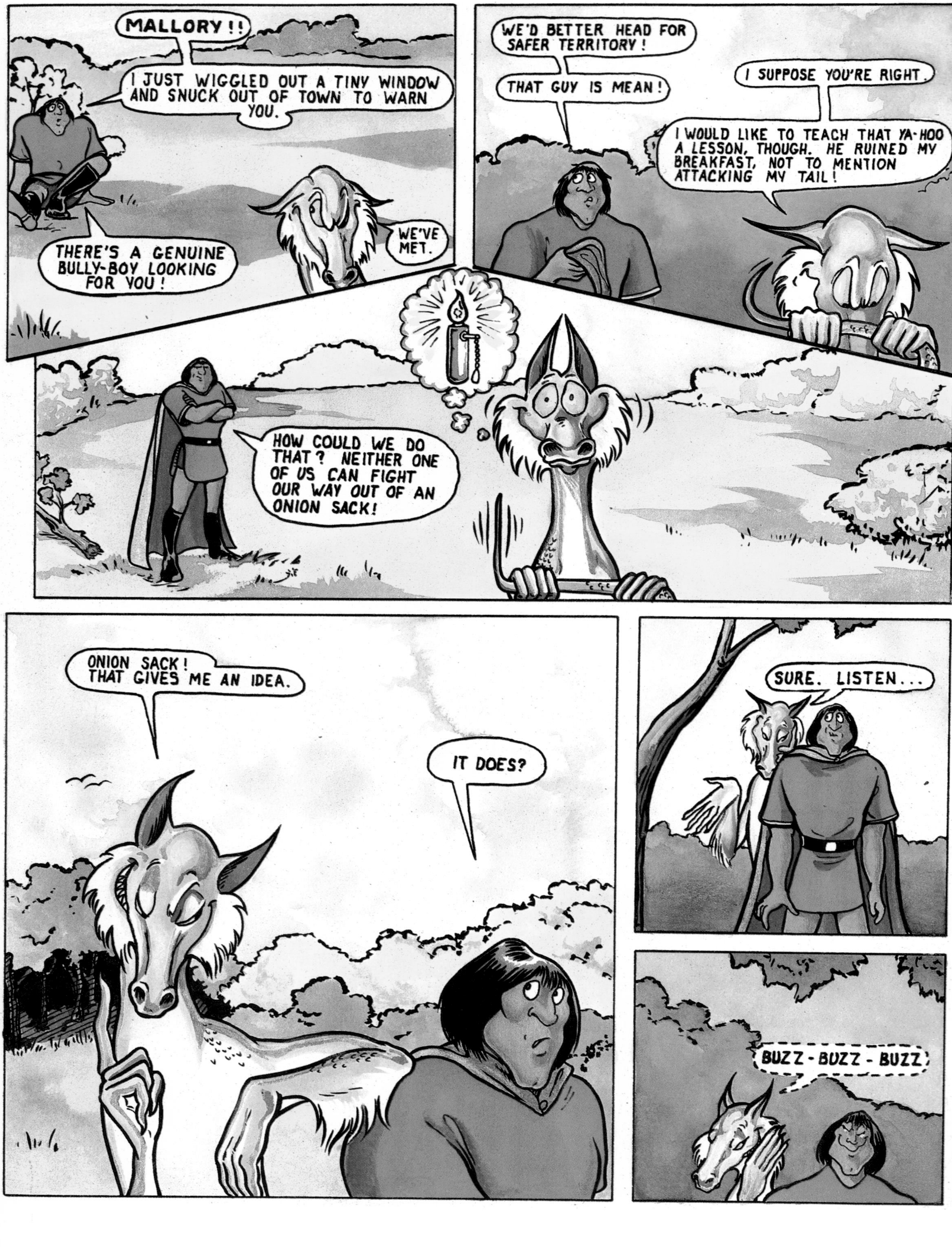
MALLORY!!
I JUST WIGGLED OUT A TINY WINDOW AND SNUCK OUT OF TOWN TO WARN YOU.
THERE'S A GENUINE BULLY-BOY LOOKING FOR YOU!
WE'VE MET.
WE'D BETTER HEAD FOR SAFER TERRITORY!
THAT GUY IS MEAN!
I SUPPOSE YOU'RE RIGHT.
I WOULD LIKE TO TEACH THAT YA-HOO A LESSON, THOUGH. HE RUINED MY BREAKFAST, NOT TO MENTION ATTACKING MY TAIL!
HOW COULD WE DO THAT? NEITHER ONE OF US CAN FIGHT OUR WAY OUT OF AN ONION SACK!
ONION SACK! THAT GIVES ME AN IDEA.
IT DOES?
SURE. LISTEN...
BUZZ-BUZZ-BUZZ

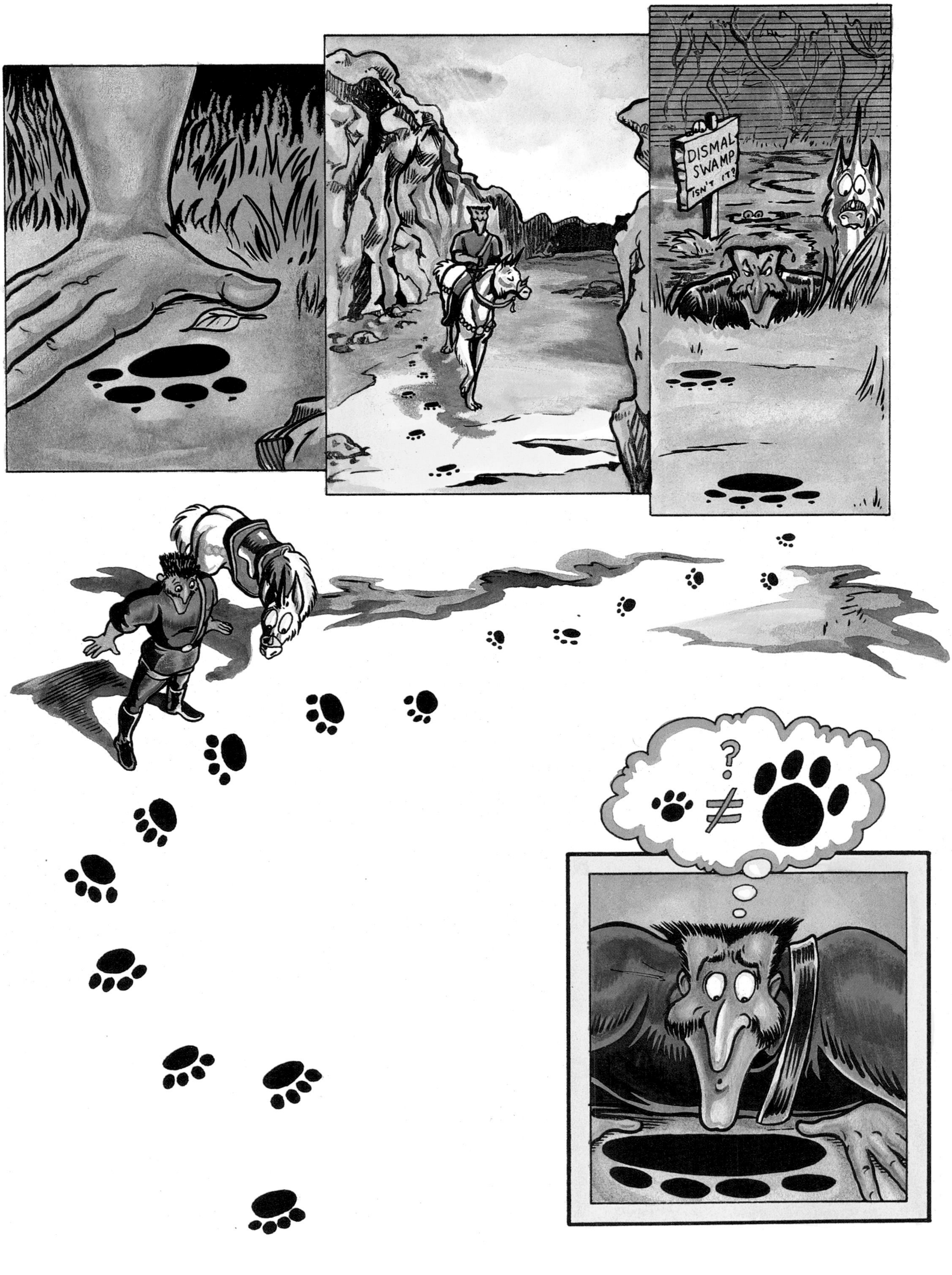
DISMAL SWAMP
ISN'T IT?

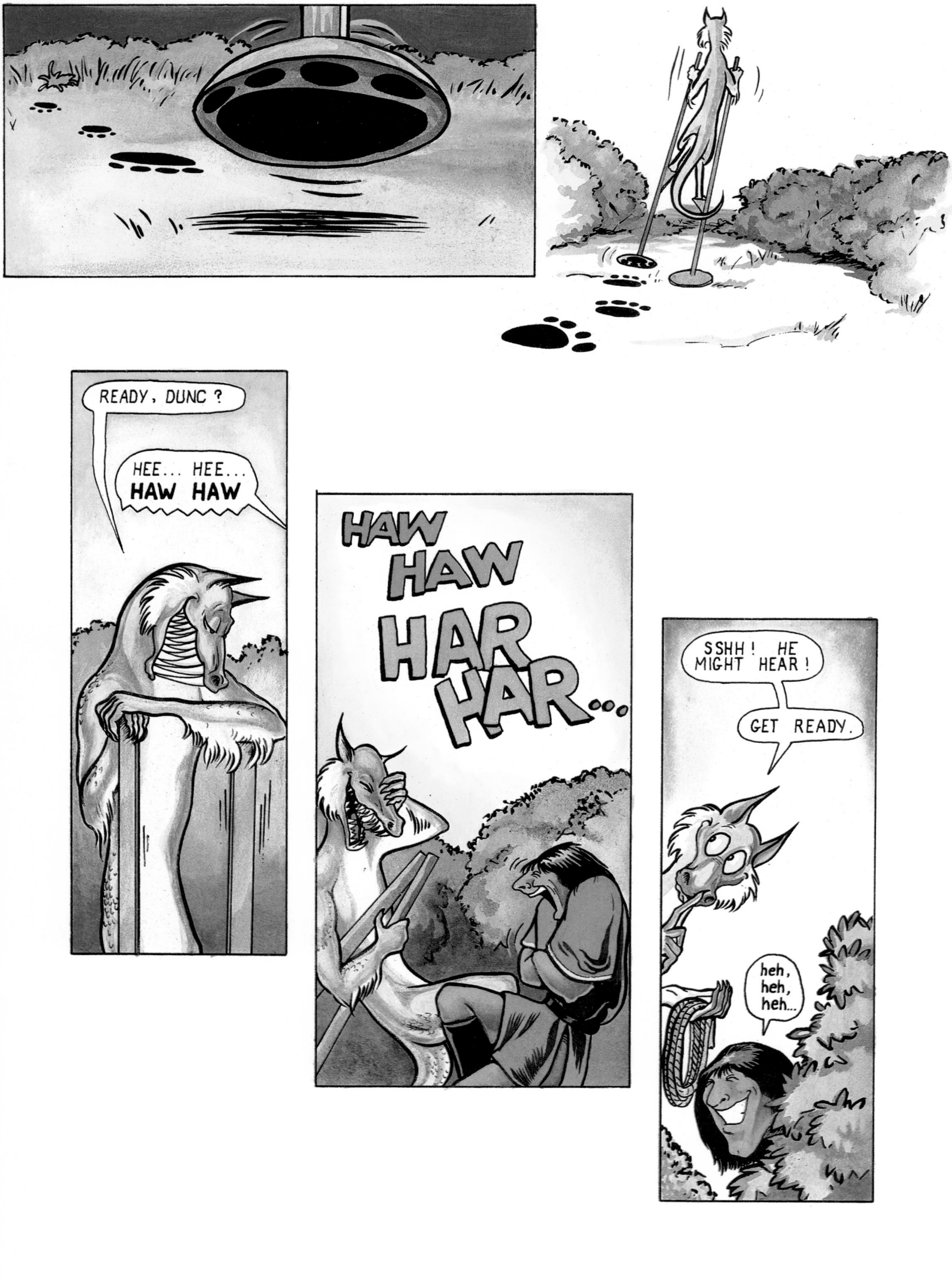

READY, DUNC?
HEE... HEE... HAW HAW
HAW HAW HAR HAR...
SSHH! HE MIGHT HEAR!
GET READY.
heh, heh, heh...

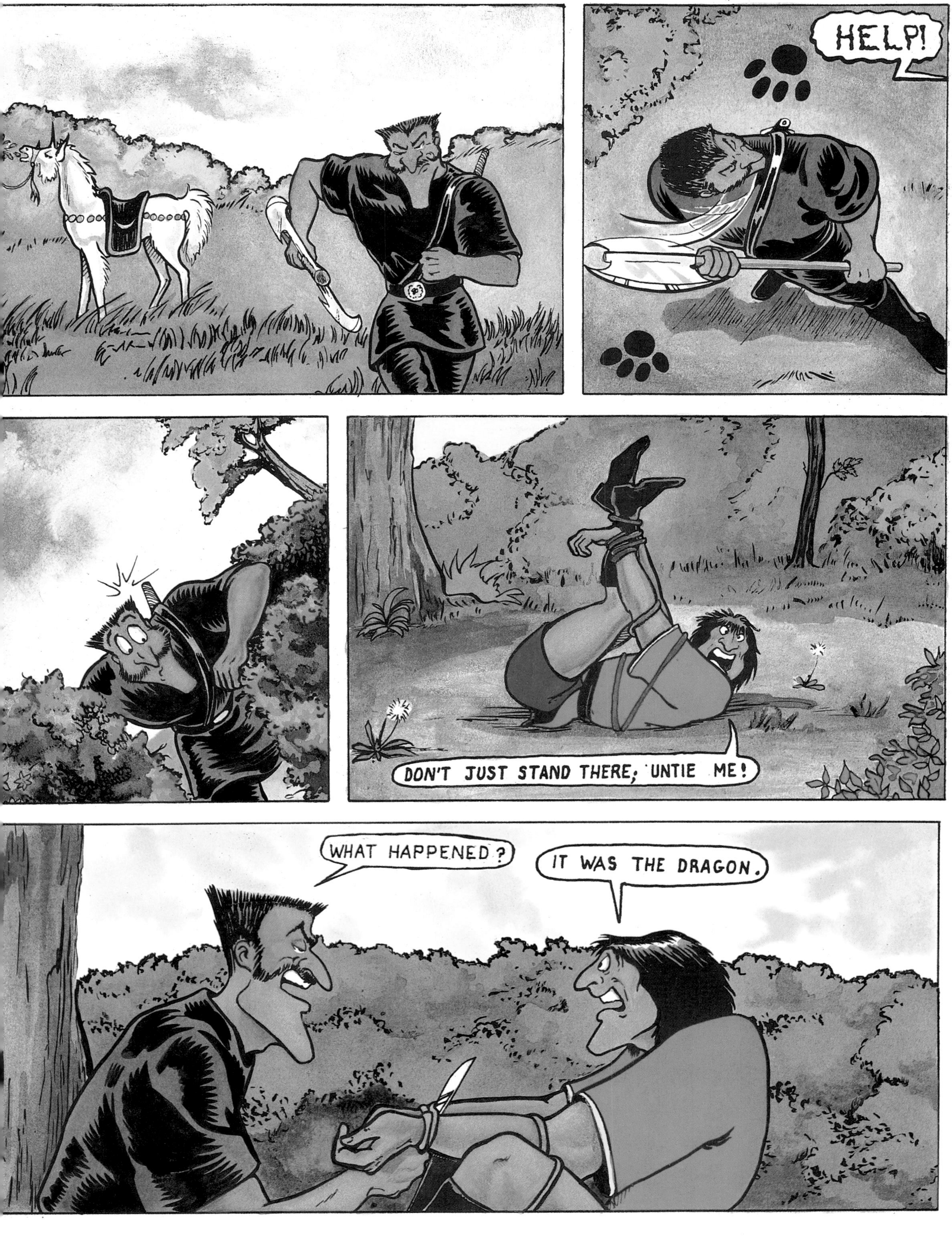
HELP!
DON'T JUST STAND THERE; UNTIE ME!
WHAT HAPPENED?
IT WAS THE DRAGON.

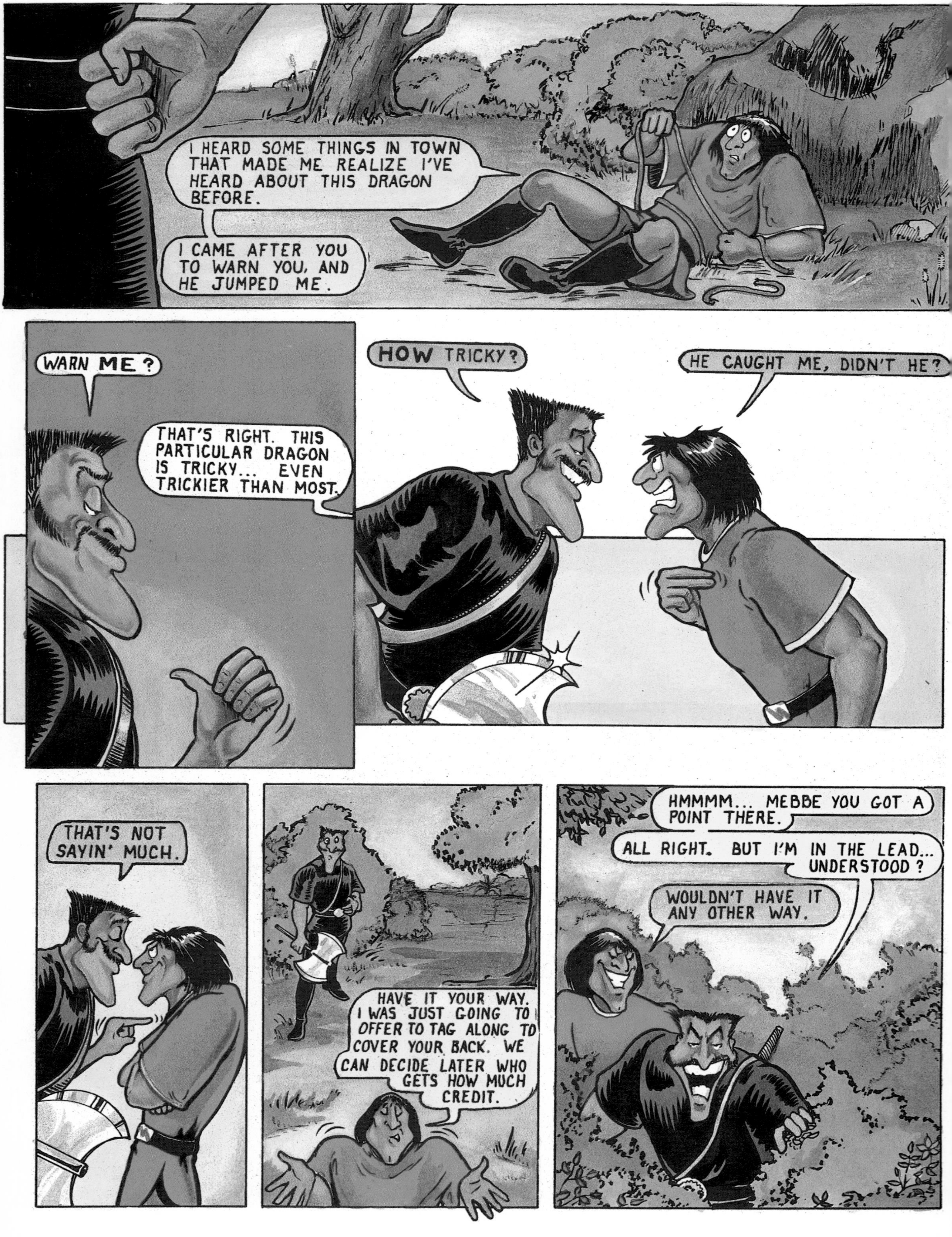
I HEARD SOME THINGS IN TOWN THAT MADE ME REALIZE I'VE HEARD ABOUT THIS DRAGON BEFORE.
I CAME AFTER YOU TO WARN YOU, AND HE JUMPED ME.
WARN ME?
THAT'S RIGHT. THIS PARTICULAR DRAGON IS TRICKY... EVEN TRICKIER THAN MOST.
HOW TRICKY?
HE CAUGHT ME, DIDN'T HE?
THAT'S NOT SAYIN' MUCH.
HAVE IT YOUR WAY. I WAS JUST GOING TO OFFER TO TAG ALONG TO COVER YOUR BACK. WE CAN DECIDE LATER WHO GETS HOW MUCH CREDIT.
HMMMM... MEBBE YOU GOT A POINT THERE.
ALL RIGHT. BUT I'M IN THE LEAD... UNDERSTOOD?
WOULDN'T HAVE IT ANY OTHER WAY.

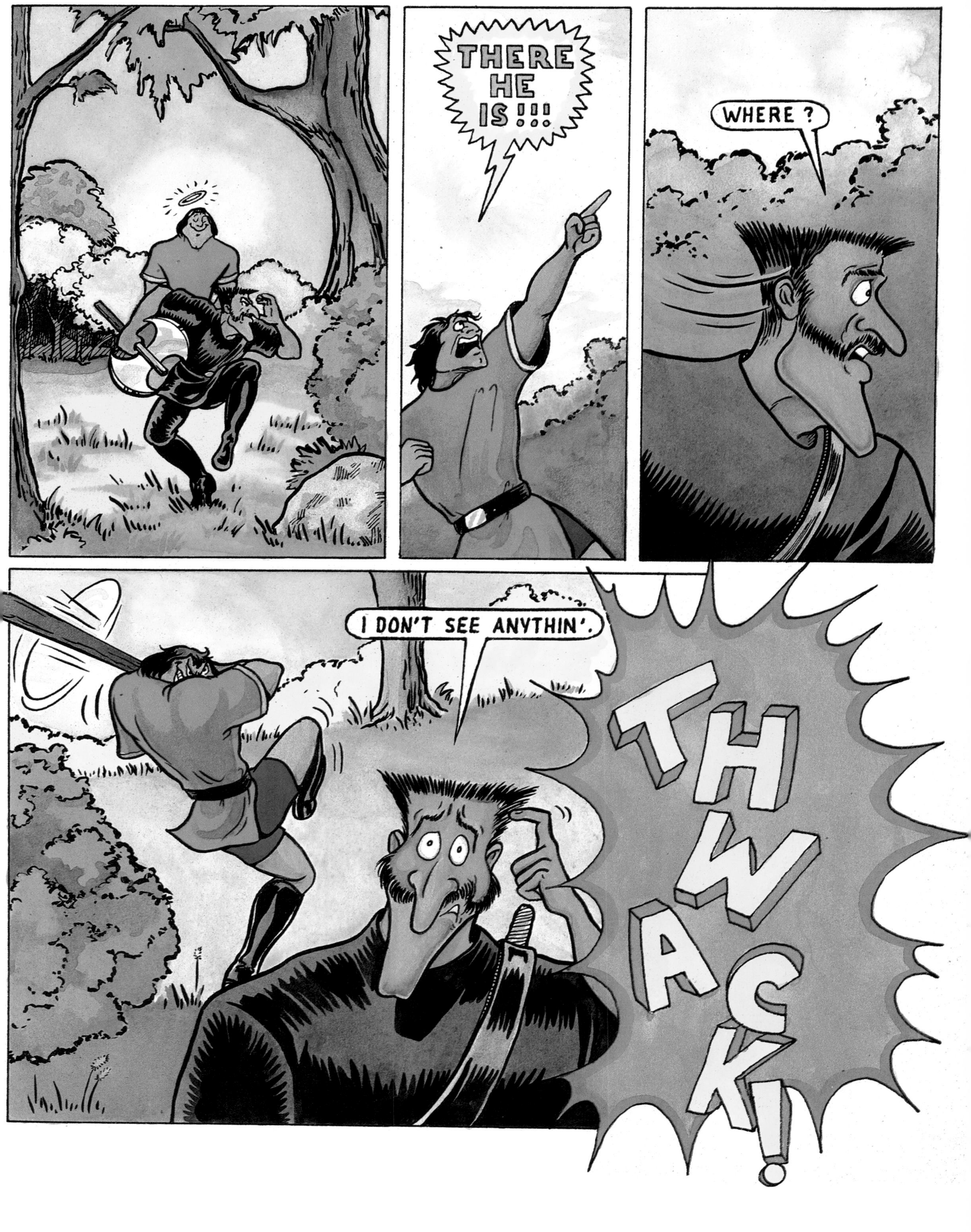
THERE HE IS!!!
WHERE ?
I DON'T SEE ANYTHIN'.
THWACK!

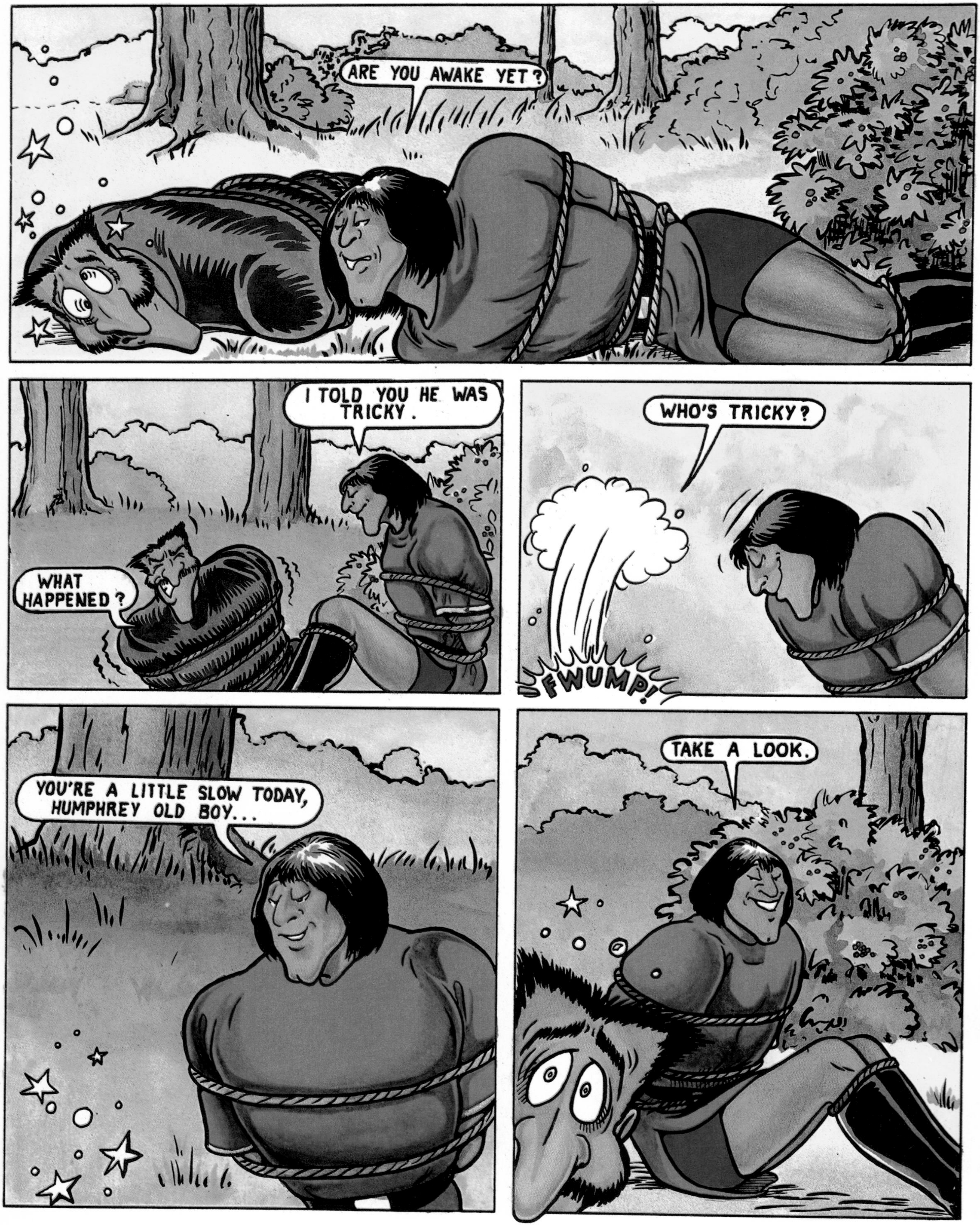
ARE YOU AWAKE YET?
I TOLD YOU HE WAS TRICKY.
WHAT HAPPENED?
WHO'S TRICKY?
FWUMP!
YOU'RE A LITTLE SLOW TODAY, HUMPHREY OLD BOY...
TAKE A LOOK.

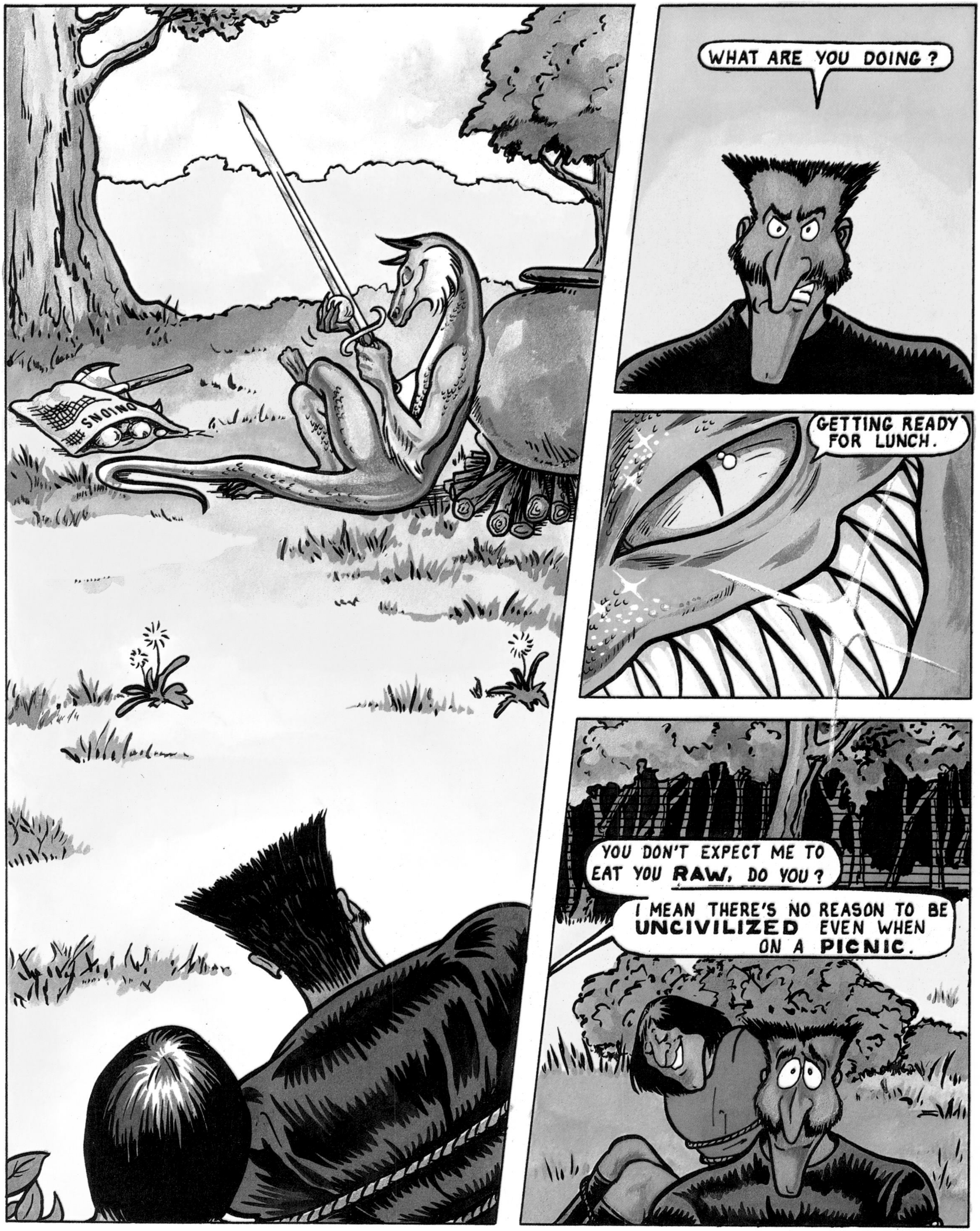
ONIONS
WHAT ARE YOU DOING?
GETTING READY FOR LUNCH.
YOU DON'T EXPECT ME TO EAT YOU RAW, DO YOU?
I MEAN THERE'S NO REASON TO BE UNCIVILIZED EVEN WHEN ON A PICNIC.

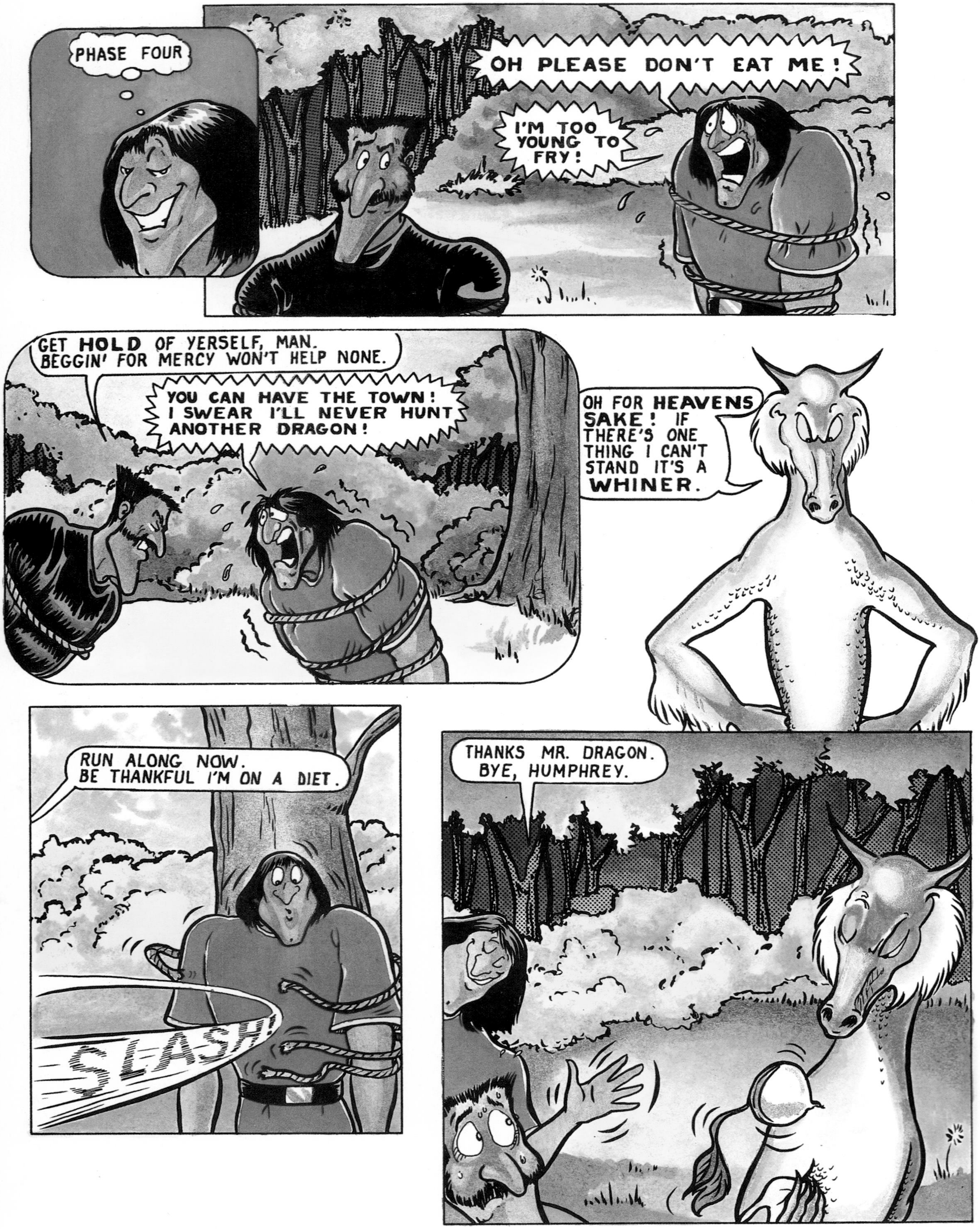
PHASE FOUR
OH PLEASE DON'T EAT ME!
I'M TOO YOUNG TO FRY!
GET HOLD OF YERSELF, MAN. BEGGIN' FOR MERCY WON'T HELP NONE.
YOU CAN HAVE THE TOWN! I SWEAR I'LL NEVER HUNT ANOTHER DRAGON!
OH FOR HEAVENS SAKE! IF THERE'S ONE THING I CAN'T STAND IT'S A WHINER.
RUN ALONG NOW. BE THANKFUL I'M ON A DIET.
SLASH!
THANKS MR. DRAGON. BYE, HUMPHREY.

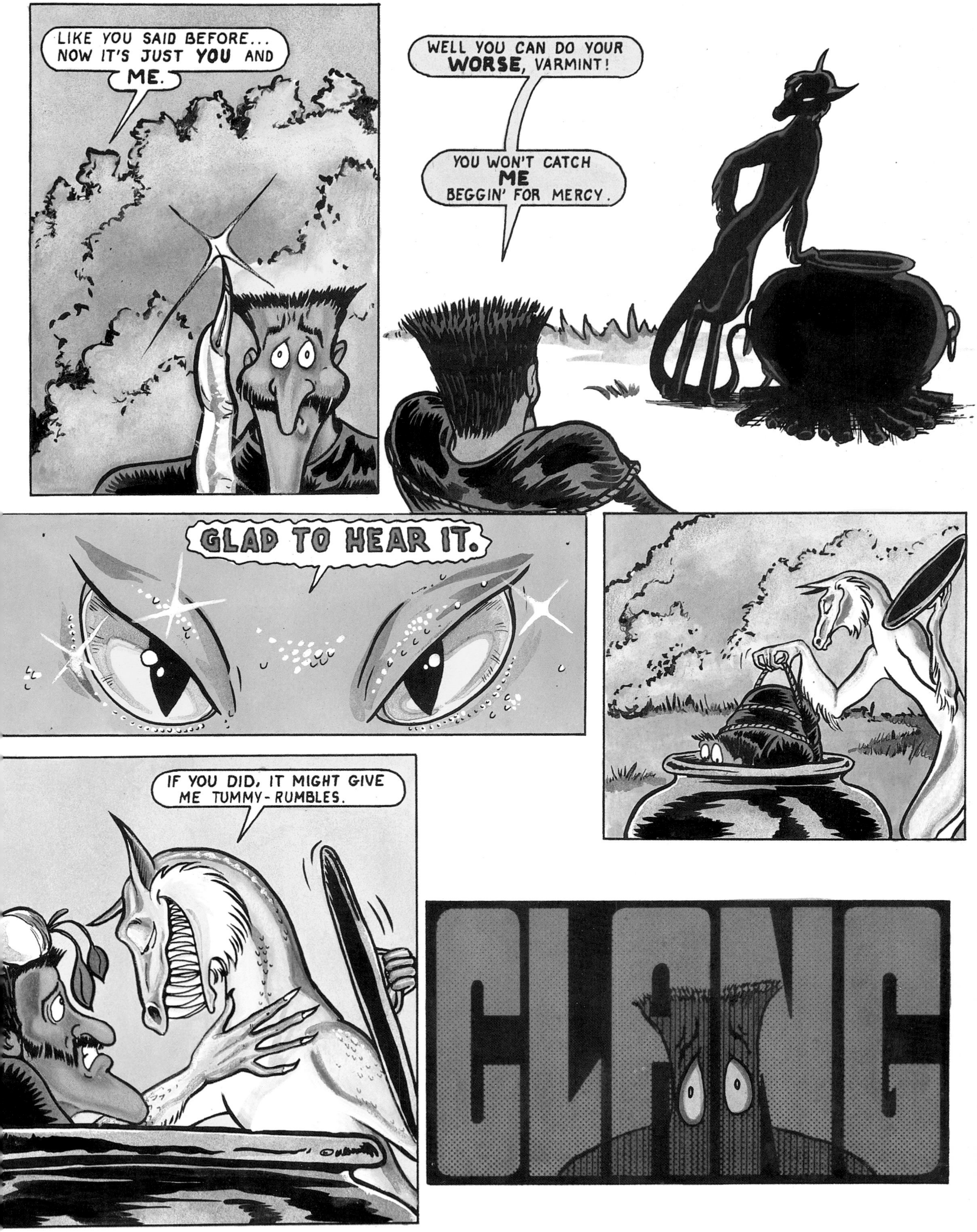
LIKE YOU SAID BEFORE... NOW IT'S JUST YOU AND ME.
WELL YOU CAN DO YOUR WORSE, VARMINT!
YOU WON'T CATCH ME BEGGIN' FOR MERCY.
GLAD TO HEAR IT.
IF YOU DID, IT MIGHT GIVE ME TUMMY-RUMBLES.
CLANG

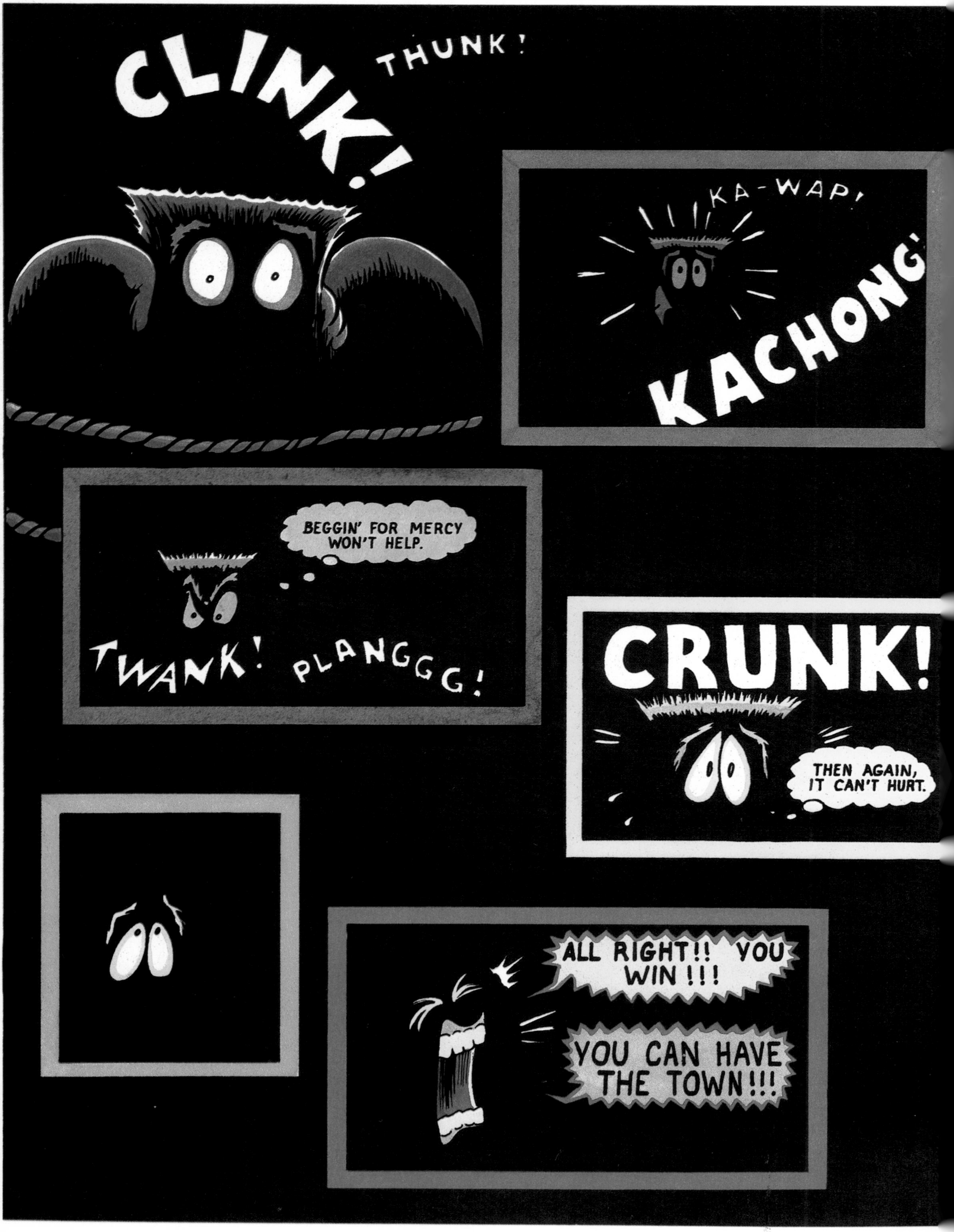
CLINK!
THUNK!
KA-WAP!
KACHONG!
BEGGIN' FOR MERCY WON'T HELP.
TWANK!
PLANGGG!
CRUNK!
THEN AGAIN, IT CAN'T HURT.
ALL RIGHT!! YOU WIN!!!
YOU CAN HAVE THE TOWN!!!

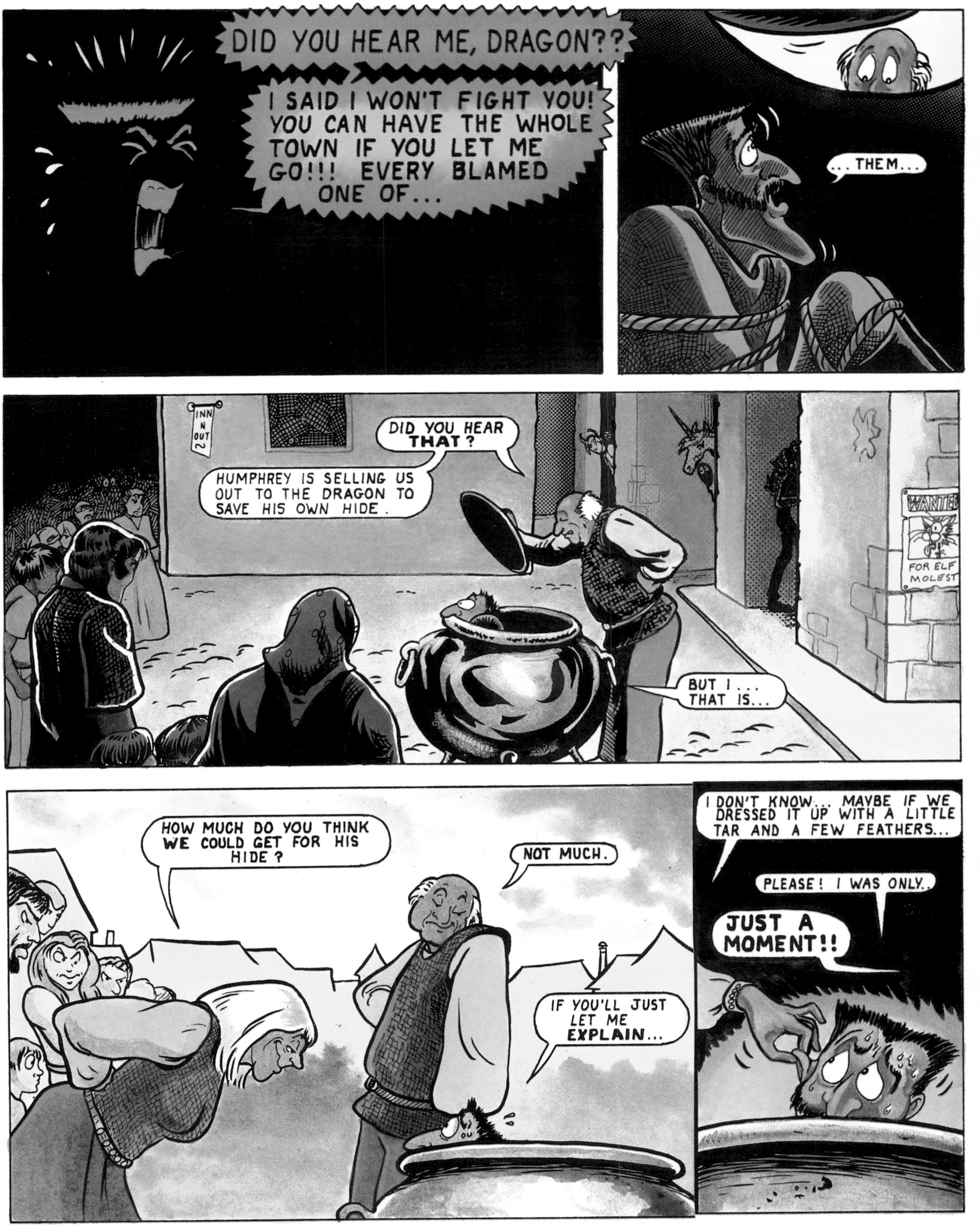
DID YOU HEAR ME, DRAGON??
I SAID I WON'T FIGHT YOU! YOU CAN HAVE THE WHOLE TOWN IF YOU LET ME GO!!! EVERY BLAMED ONE OF...
...THEM...
INN N OUT
DID YOU HEAR THAT?
HUMPHREY IS SELLING US OUT TO THE DRAGON TO SAVE HIS OWN HIDE.
WANTED
FOR ELF MOLEST
BUT I... THAT IS...
HOW MUCH DO YOU THINK WE COULD GET FOR HIS HIDE?
NOT MUCH.
IF YOU'LL JUST LET ME EXPLAIN...
I DON'T KNOW... MAYBE IF WE DRESSED IT UP WITH A LITTLE TAR AND A FEW FEATHERS...
PLEASE! I WAS ONLY..
JUST A MOMENT!!

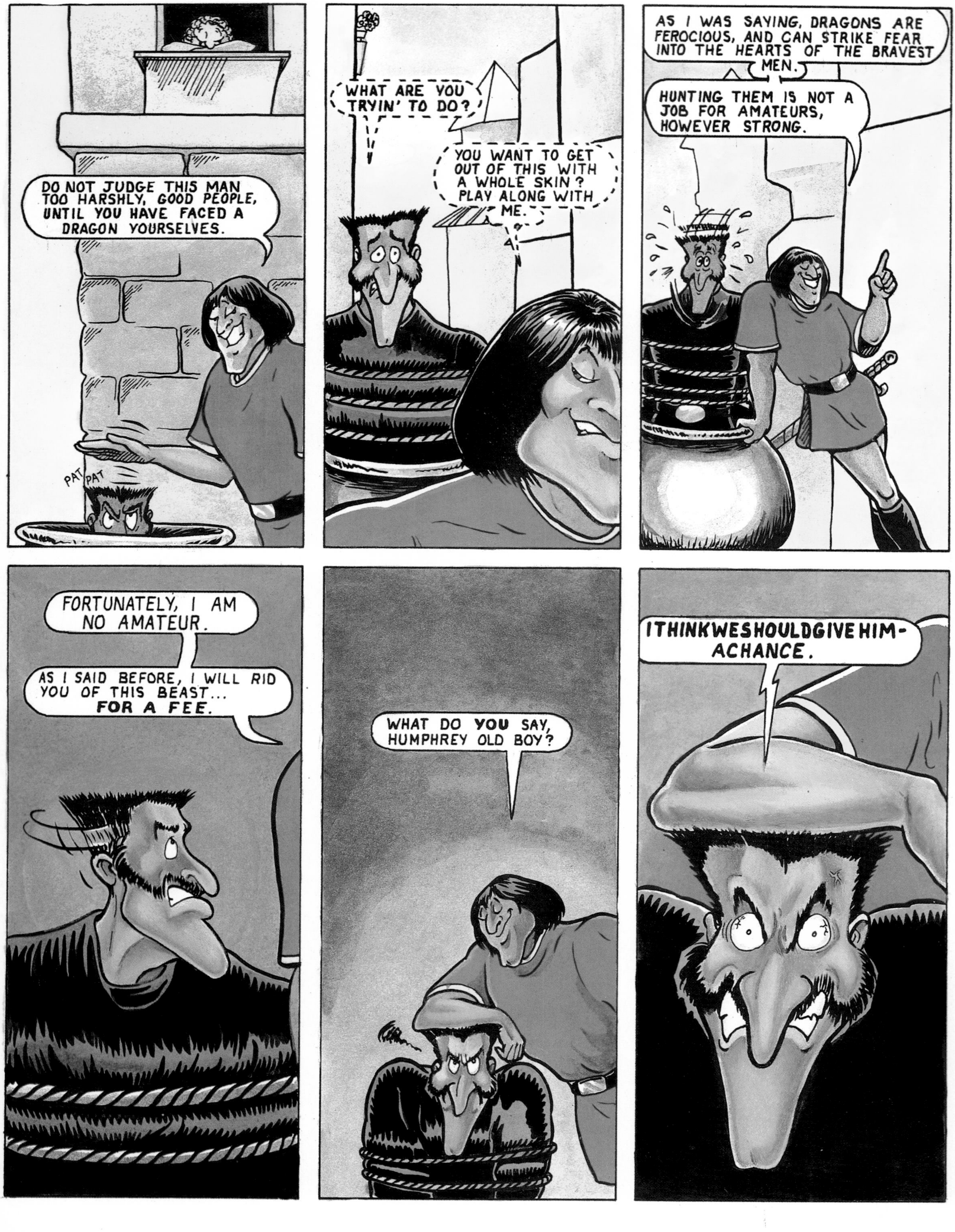
DO NOT JUDGE THIS MAN TOO HARSHLY, GOOD PEOPLE, UNTIL YOU HAVE FACED A DRAGON YOURSELVES.
PAT PAT
WHAT ARE YOU TRYIN' TO DO?
YOU WANT TO GET OUT OF THIS WITH A WHOLE SKIN? PLAY ALONG WITH ME.
AS I WAS SAYING, DRAGONS ARE FEROCIOUS, AND CAN STRIKE FEAR INTO THE HEARTS OF THE BRAVEST MEN.
HUNTING THEM IS NOT A JOB FOR AMATEURS, HOWEVER STRONG.
FORTUNATELY, I AM NO AMATEUR.
AS I SAID BEFORE, I WILL RID YOU OF THIS BEAST... **FOR A FEE.**
WHAT DO **YOU** SAY, HUMPHREY OLD BOY?
ITHINKWESHOULDGIVEHIM-ACHANCE.

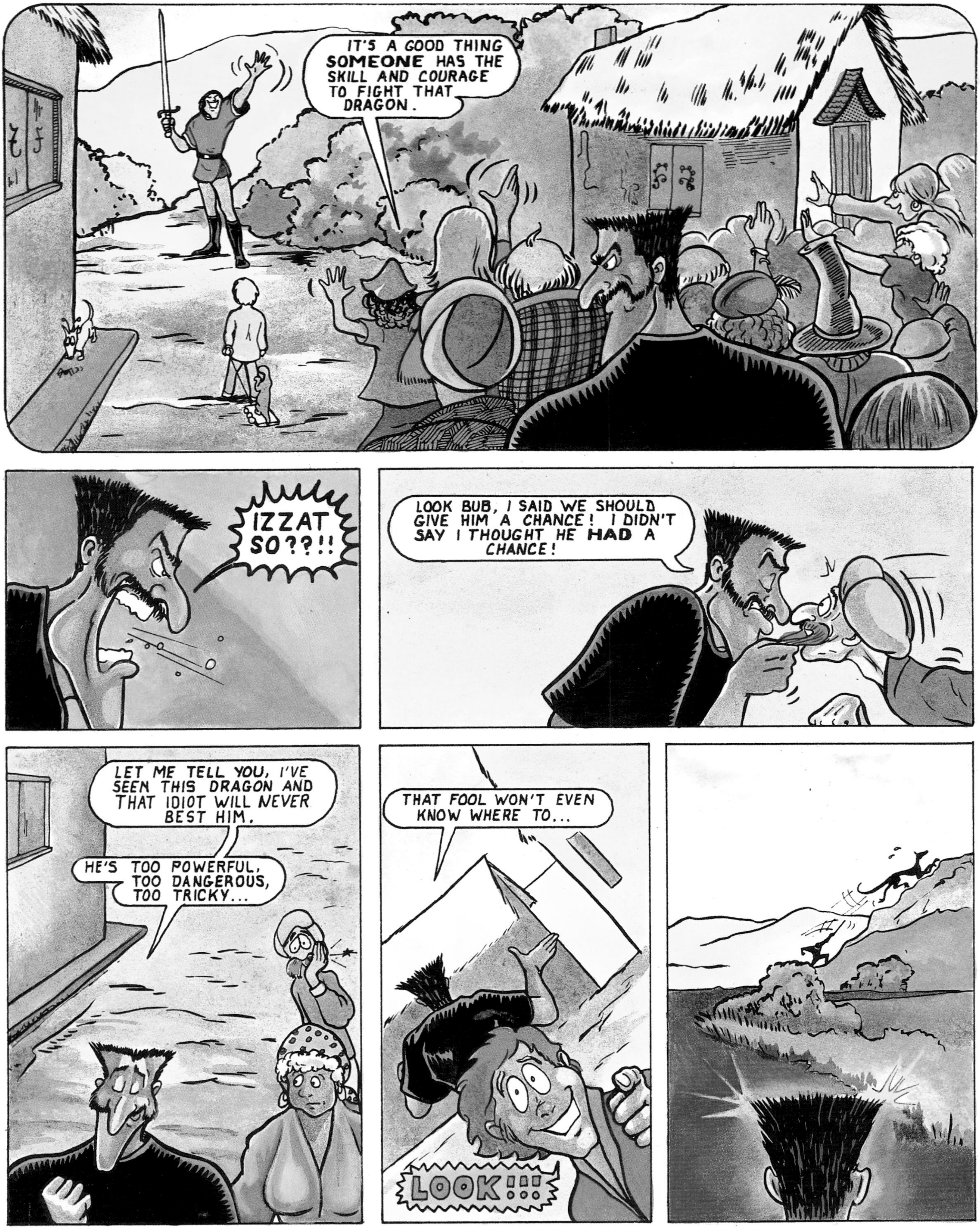
IT'S A GOOD THING SOMEONE HAS THE SKILL AND COURAGE TO FIGHT THAT DRAGON.
IZZAT SO??!!
LOOK BUB, I SAID WE SHOULD GIVE HIM A CHANCE! I DIDN'T SAY I THOUGHT HE HAD A CHANCE!
LET ME TELL YOU, I'VE SEEN THIS DRAGON AND THAT IDIOT WILL NEVER BEST HIM.
HE'S TOO POWERFUL, TOO DANGEROUS, TOO TRICKY...
THAT FOOL WON'T EVEN KNOW WHERE TO...
LOOK!!!

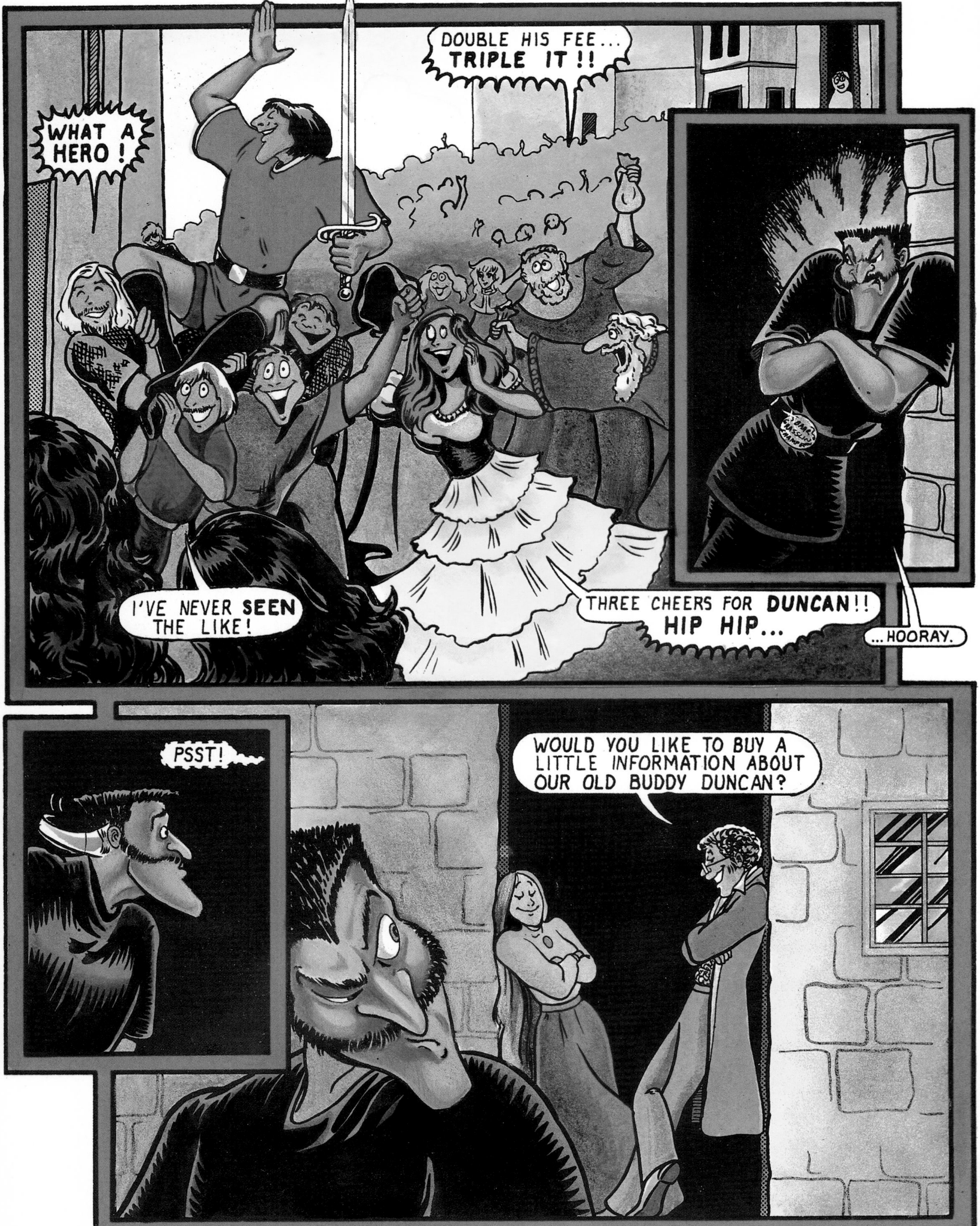

WHAT A HERO!
DOUBLE HIS FEE... TRIPLE IT!!
I'VE NEVER SEEN THE LIKE!
THREE CHEERS FOR DUNCAN!! HIP HIP...
...HOORAY.
PSST!
WOULD YOU LIKE TO BUY A LITTLE INFORMATION ABOUT OUR OLD BUDDY DUNCAN?

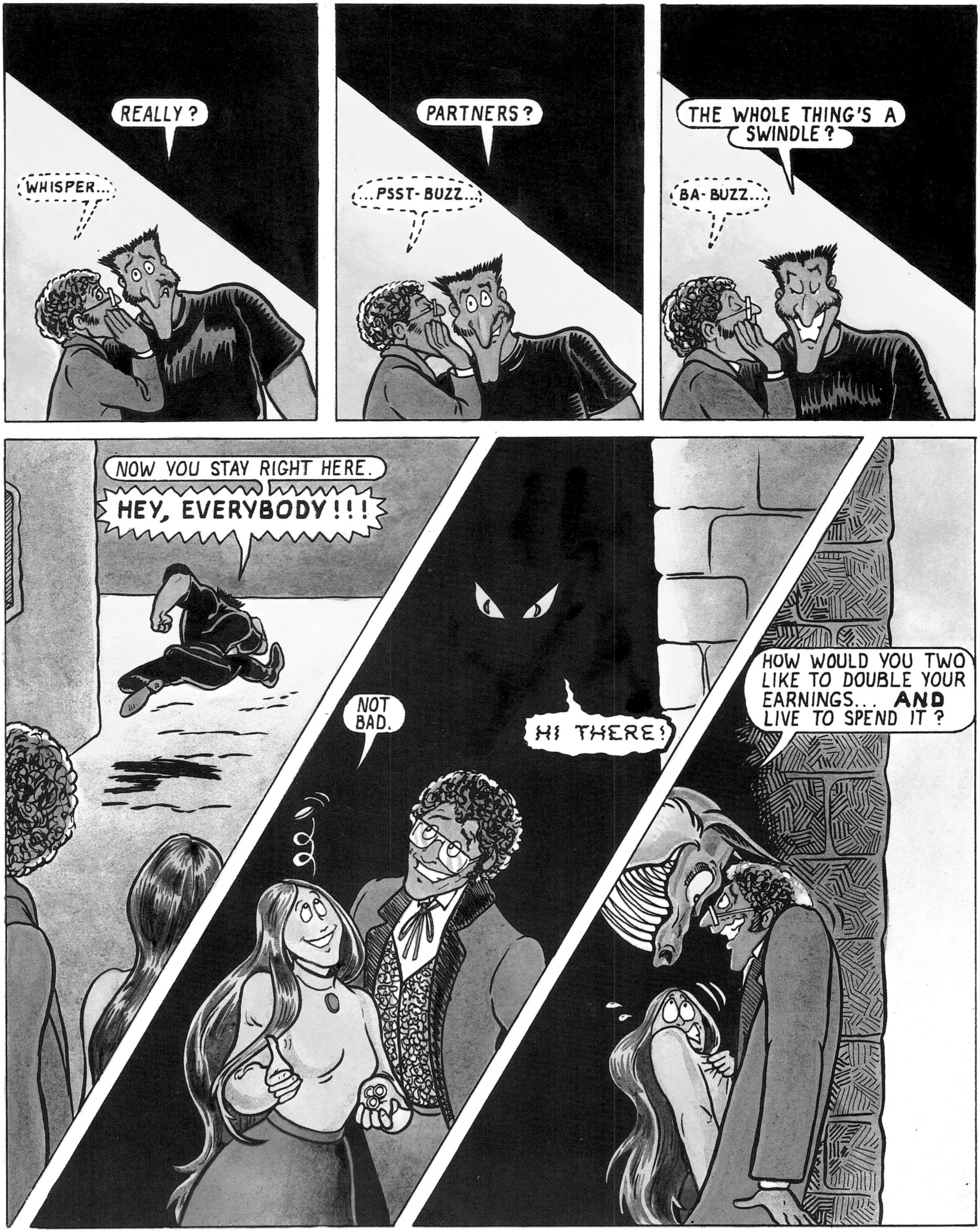
WHISPER...
REALLY?
...PSST-BUZZ...
PARTNERS?
BA-BUZZ....
THE WHOLE THING'S A SWINDLE?
NOW YOU STAY RIGHT HERE.
HEY, EVERYBODY!!!
NOT BAD.
HI THERE!
HOW WOULD YOU TWO LIKE TO DOUBLE YOUR EARNINGS... AND LIVE TO SPEND IT?

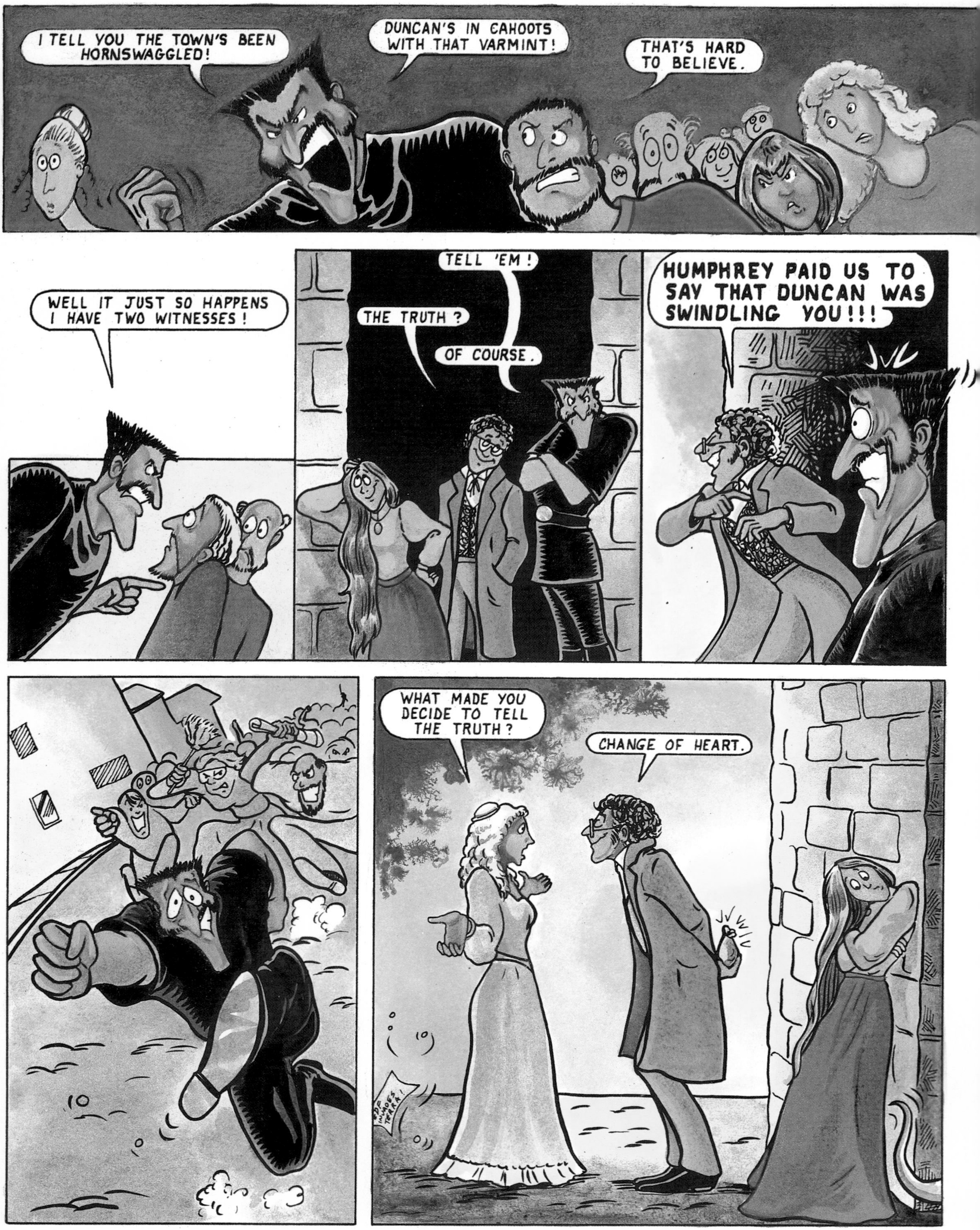
I TELL YOU THE TOWN'S BEEN HORNSWAGGLED!
DUNCAN'S IN CAHOOTS WITH THAT VARMINT!
THAT'S HARD TO BELIEVE.
WELL IT JUST SO HAPPENS I HAVE TWO WITNESSES!
TELL 'EM!
THE TRUTH?
OF COURSE.
HUMPHREY PAID US TO SAY THAT DUNCAN WAS SWINDLING YOU!!!
WHAT MADE YOU DECIDE TO TELL THE TRUTH?
CHANGE OF HEART.

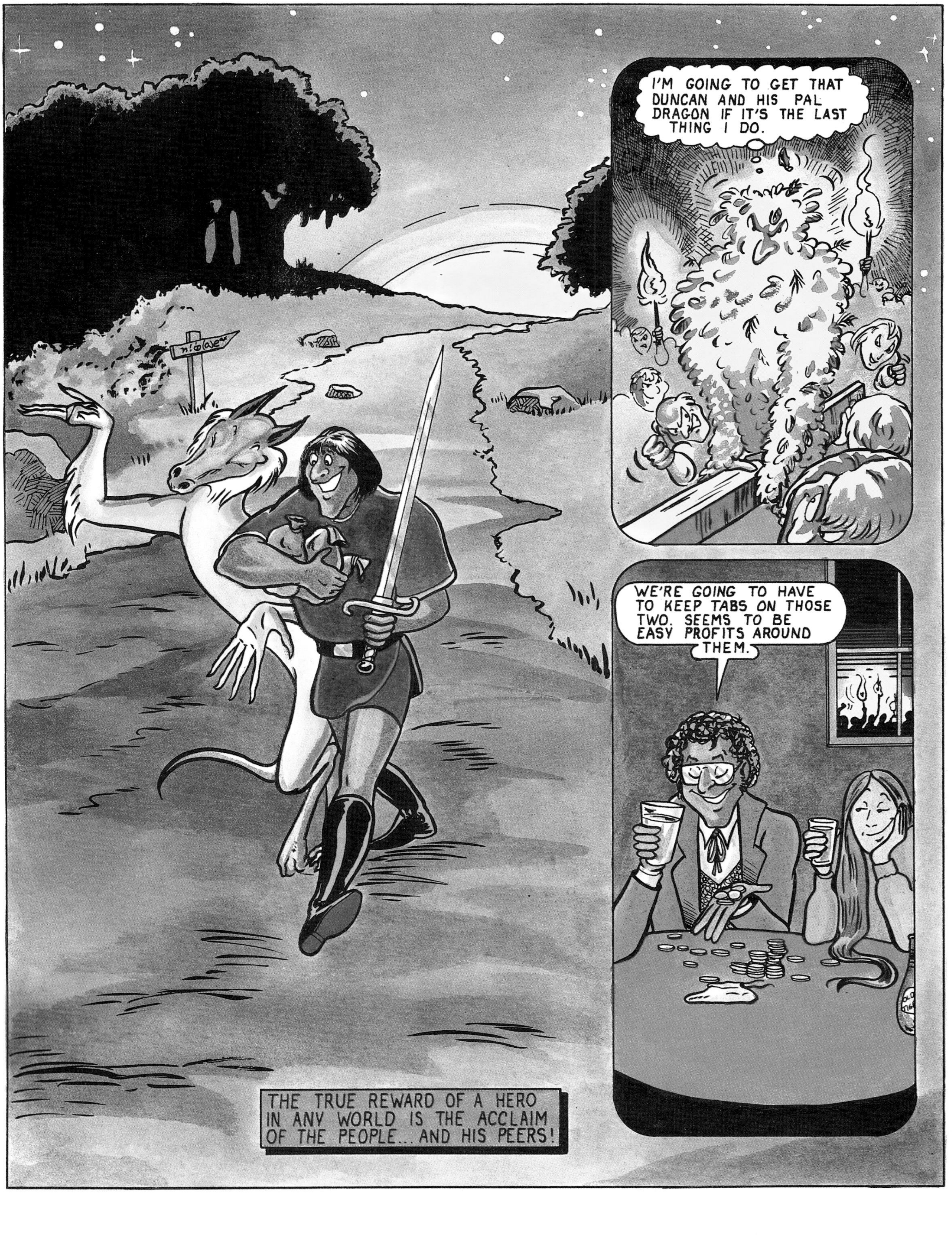

I'M GOING TO GET THAT DUNCAN AND HIS PAL DRAGON IF IT'S THE LAST THING I DO.
WE'RE GOING TO HAVE TO KEEP TABS ON THOSE TWO. SEEMS TO BE EASY PROFITS AROUND THEM.
THE TRUE REWARD OF A HERO IN ANY WORLD IS THE ACCLAIM OF THE PEOPLE... AND HIS PEERS!

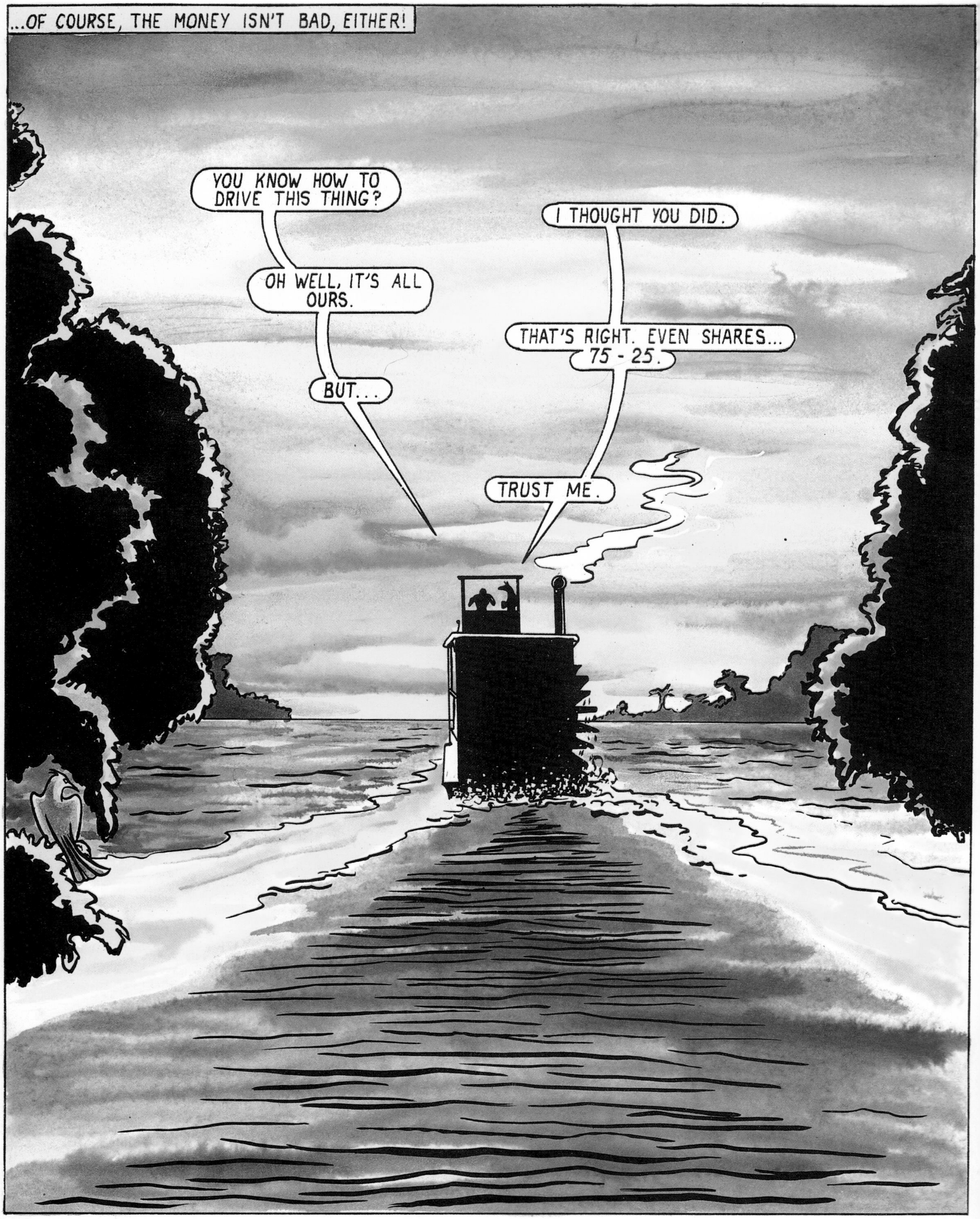
...OF COURSE, THE MONEY ISN'T BAD, EITHER!
YOU KNOW HOW TO DRIVE THIS THING?
I THOUGHT YOU DID.
OH WELL, IT'S ALL OURS.
THAT'S RIGHT. EVEN SHARES... 75 - 25.
BUT...
TRUST ME.

Duncan & Mallory
will
return in

THE
BAR-NONE
RANCH

This graphic novel series
is published semiannually by
Starblaze Graphics.

AFTERWORDS

Where do we creative types get our ideas? Well, this one started with a gag-postcard Mel. White sent me back in '84. Now I've known and admired Mel.'s work for years, so the fact that the card was funny and clever came as no surprise, but something caught my eye. This piece depicted a card game. Seated at the table were a dragon, a brawny knight (who was obviously losing), and a scared kid with a unicorn looking over his shoulder. The kid and the knight I had seen before (at one time Mel. showed me her concepts of characters from the *Myth Adventures* books), but the dragon...

This is what started it all.

He was about eight feet high instead of huge or tiny, had a prehensile tail, and a sly expression instead of fierce, dense, or stupid...in short, I fell in love with him on sight. I wouldn't have believed that at this late date in fantasy it would have been possible to come up with an original dragon, but Mel. had done it!

With my usual flair for procrastination, I didn't do anything about it until the next time I saw Mel. at a convention.

"Hey, Mel.!" I greeted her. "Loved the dragon on the card! What are you going to do with him?"

"Huh?" she replied in that cute way she has.

"You know...greeting cards, comic scripts, animated cartoon shows, pot holders, that kind of thing!"

As it turned out, she didn't have any plans to develop the character and wasn't sure what I meant about building stories around him, so I led her through the exercise: He's going to need someone else to interact with to get away from internal monologues...and a villain or two for conflict, ongoing ones are best since you don't have to keep coming up with new ones to introduce to the reader (like the Beagle Boys in Uncle Scrooge).

She got the hang of the game in no time flat, and in half an hour, the basics of **Duncan and Mallory** started to take shape. Since then it's been smooth sailing all the way.

Right.

Once Mel. and I were on board with Donning/Starblaze and ready to go, you would think getting the rest of the creative team together would be a snap. Well, it was—sort of.

Close your eyes and imagine a graphic creative team. Got it? There they are, gathered around the drawing boards in their studio/office, brainstorming ideas and critiquing each others' efforts. It's a great picture, but totally inaccurate in this case.

The **Duncan and Mallory** creative team is scattered, geographically and mentally. None of them has the luxury of working on this project full time.

Robert Asprin is based in Ann Arbor, Michigan but is seldom home due to his heavy convention traveling schedule. As writer/editor, he is responsible for a number of projects: the **Thieves' World** anthologies from Ace, **Thieves' World Graphics** from Donning/Starblaze, as well as the **Myth Adventures** series of novels and graphics. In his previous "spare time" back in his bean-counting days for Xerox, Inc., Asprin wrote novels like **Bug Wars, Tambu, Cold Cash War** and **Mirror Friend, Mirror Foe** (this last one with George Takei).

Mel. White hails from the Dallas/ Fort Worth metroplex and comes by her insanity legitimately...she's the mother of two. She programs and installs computers and for laughs, pencils **Duncan and Mallory** (although sometimes that laugh is dangerously close to a hysterical screech. However....)

Colleen Winters, from Pennsylvania, handles the inks. She is currently a full-time student pursuing her master's in information sciences. Her experiences with the **Duncan and Mallory** creative team have inspired her to devote her life to a sincere attempt to create artificial intelligence.

Jane Fancher provides our color from the state of Washington and is the only full-time professional artist on the team. You may remember Jane's colors on **ElfQuest Books 2** and **3.** She also adapted, penciled, inked, and even lettered her own independently published comic version of C. J. Cherryh's **The Gate of Ivrel.** You'll be seeing more of Jane's colors in **Fortune's Friends: Hell Week** from Donning/Starblaze as well as the continuation of her own special project.

Johnny Amburn, our letterer, is a west Texan. As far as dubious backgrounds go, I think all we need say is that he is currently working as an engineer for Southwestern Bell.

All we have left to say now is that we hope you enjoyed the book. Thanks for looking us over.

—Robert Asprin and
Mel. White
August 1986